CASTING SHADOWS

WORD MACHINE PRESS

Find out more about Word Machine Press:
Blog: wordmachinepress.wordpress.com
Twitter: WMachinePress
FB: Word-Machine-Press

CASTING SHADOWS

EXTRAORDINARY TALES FROM NEW WRITERS

WORDMACHINE
PRESS

Published in 2013 by Word Machine Press
using SilverWood Books Empowered Publishing®

30 Queen Charlotte Street, Bristol, BS1 4HJ
www.silverwoodbooks.co.uk

Text copyright © Word Machine Press 2013

The right of Word Machine Press to be identified as the author
of this work has been asserted by them in accordance
with the Copyright, Designs and Patents Act 1988.

ISBN 978-1-78132-148-5 (paperback)
ISBN 978-1-78132-149-2 (hardback)
ISBN 978-1-78132-150-8 (ebook)

British Library Cataloguing in Publication Data
A CIP catalogue record for this book is available from the British Library

Set in Sabon by SilverWood Books
Printed on responsibly sourced paper

Contents

Foreword

When I was asked to write a foreword for a book of ghost stories, I said yes at once. I love spooky stories, and I had heard that this collection was particularly good. I know from experience that short stories of any sort, and ghost stories in particular, are incredibly difficult to write, so I was fascinated to see how these new writers had pulled it off. I knew that this project came out of an assignment for a Professional Writing MA course, but that everyone suddenly realised they ought to be published. They now seem to have an unstoppable momentum, and with good reason: this is a remarkable collection of masterful tales.

A ghost story seems like a straightforward thing to write: its structure, to a point, is fixed: things are likely to start off in a creepy version of normality, the reader constantly wondering what is really happening, then become mysterious and troubling, with a final twist or reveal that will, ideally, both surprise the reader and make the hairs on their arms stand up on end.

Actually achieving this in a way that will take the reader by surprise takes a deceptive amount of skill and planning.

These eight stories have pulled it off admirably. I was not expecting every single one of them to make me shiver, to produce that satisfying 'oh my God!' moment. But they all do. Their variety of different settings, from Bali to the Stocksbridge bypass, and the different forms the other-worldliness takes, means that this collection pulls the reader along at a breakneck speed. A traveller stumbles into a clifftop pub in the mist.

A woman lives surrounded by her ex's clutter. A disliked granny arrives in the family home to die. As soon as I was into one world, it was gone. I was ready to plunge straight into the next.

One of the joys of unsettling stories such as these is the imbuing of everyday objects with creepiness. I loved the way things like a porcelain jug shaped like a cow, vomiting milk, became suddenly terrifying. A forget-me-not wedding ring is crucial to one story, terraced rice paddies in Indonesia to another. This twisting of everyday life into creepy suspense is in the tradition of the very best horror writing, by authors from Daphne du Maurier to Stephen King.

Having read these stories I am now profoundly unnerved. I read the last in the collection aloud to my nine-year-old son, when he asked what I was doing. He shivered and giggled and said: 'that is a great book'. I agree with him. This collection is a wonderful, invigorating read: I look forward to seeing what these writers will do next.

Emily Barr 2013

Vivienne

C H Anderson

My therapist said I should try to recall everything that happened: she thinks it'll help me come to terms with it all. I've always kept a journal. I wrote about it there first – while it was fresh in my mind. Before I knew what was going to happen. It helps me remember, keep things clear in my head. So here it is, all of it…

I met Vivienne a couple of years ago. She had just moved here from France on a gap year. She was so beautiful and funny and smart. We got on really well from the get go, like a house on fire, people said. I knew she was going to go back to university in France, she'd said so from the very start. Med school: she was going to be a doctor. I fell in love with her. We were together almost the whole time she was here and I adored every minute of it, even though I knew it would end.

She had this red dress, with little white polka-dots and she wore it all the time, especially in the summer. She's wearing it in my favourite picture, sitting on a fence in the countryside in that red dress and big green wellies. Vivi was an old-fashioned kind of girl, all about phone booths and writing letters. I tried to get her into social media but she was stubborn. She said we'd keep in touch by writing letters and sending photos of how we are getting on, that sort of thing.

When she left that afternoon a year ago today, we didn't really say goodbye: we agreed there was no good in it – too final and too painful. We just hugged and that was that. She promised me that she'd call me from the airport when her flight landed. I'd waved her goodbye, smiling, hiding from her how upset I was. The flat was so empty without all her stuff and I sat there in the dark, waiting for her to call. I missed her so much. Hell, I still do.

She did call. I remember because I nearly missed it and her end was loud with other voices, a background of airport bustle.

I had to ask her to repeat herself. She said that she was staying at her mum's house until she moved into her student residence. She said she missed me and she'd call soon and then hung up, just like that, just like always.

A few weeks later, still no phone call. I assumed she was busy. I'd called her a couple of times but it just rang out. Perhaps she'd get back to me when she had some free time, y'know, post an address to me or something.

That's when the dreams started – vivid and weird. It started with crows, just a bunch of crows sitting on power lines, which was fine except for the feeling. The image was accompanied by a sudden feeling of deep unease and I'd wake up. I had that same dream every few nights for a long time. It always started with the crows and then stuff got added for a while until the picture seemed to be complete. So there were these creepy crows lined up on a telephone line and a building on fire. Vivienne was there standing in her red dress. In the dream it was raining but it wasn't water. It looked like snow but it was flower petals. Little white petals, mixed with little flecks of ash.

I was never much of a dreamer so it was particularly strange for me to remember this so vividly. I wasn't getting much sleep though so I chalked it up to waking up so early. Y'know, they say if you are woken up suddenly you'll remember the dream better than if you wake up naturally but to be honest, I'm not so sure that that was it.

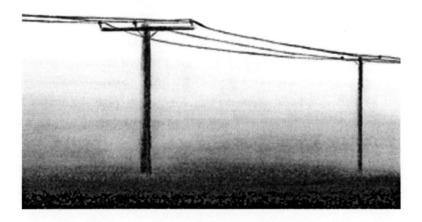

13

I went out with friends, drank a lot, tried to get those dreams out of my head and stop thinking about Vivi. So, one day I met up with my mates, just went to the pub to watch the game, Villa vs Arsenal. They'd all known Vivi too. See, when she'd first arrived she didn't really know anyone, she just liked the idea of living in London. She had happened to walk into the same bar as me and we'd got talking. I was out with them that night as well. They all seemed to get on well.

So, anyway, we were in the pub, again. It was already dark out and drizzly. I won't deny that I'd had my fair share of pints but I swear that I saw her. Only from behind, but it was definitely her, Vivienne, in that bright dress. She walked away out of the pub. I got up and ran after her but it was crowded and I must've missed her because when I got out into the street and looked around, she was gone.

One of my friends asked if I was ok. He must have followed me because he was standing behind me in the doorway. I told him straight out. He just stared at me and suggested that I go home and get some rest.

I had the dream again that night. It seemed more real than before. I could almost feel the heat from the flames and the soft petals brushing against my skin.

I saw her again and again over the coming weeks: in a café, at the tube station, or even just walking around in the street. I told myself that I must just be imagining it: I missed her, and our flat seemed so lonely without her.

By this point, I'd come to the conclusion that she wanted nothing to do with me and I was falling apart wanting to see her or even hear from her. I'd only glimpsed her from a distance. Red is not an uncommon colour for women to wear. I just needed to get some sleep and get over her and it would all be fine. But it still hurt. No matter how much I told myself that it didn't.

That night I went out to a New Year's party. It was at a fancy hotel, a friend-of-a-friend invite thing. I was reluctant but didn't want to be a total liability, so I went. It was actually a lot of fun for the first few hours. I didn't drink much so my mind was relatively clear and I saw her. This time was different. This was clear as day. She was so close, not six feet away from me, coat on and ready to leave. She looked great, healthy and happy, just like when we were together. Again, like every time I'd seen her recently, she was always on her way out. I followed her. This time I called out her name but she ignored me, like she didn't even hear me.

I got angry. She was back from France, if she had gone at all, and she didn't even have the guts or decency to tell me. She had ignored me, like I was worth nothing to her. I had tried to call her again that day but I couldn't get through. I had decided that she'd probably changed her number or something. I had lost sight of her. It always seemed like I was a few steps behind her. I promised myself that the next time I saw her, I'd catch her and talk to her. I needed answers.

I didn't see her again for a couple of months – probably because I didn't really leave the house much. I got a commission so I stayed in and worked. The nightmares didn't stop though. They flooded back from time to time, to remind me of her, hinting that she was around, doing great without me and I thought I heard her sometimes, inside my head. Just talking or laughing, laughing at me.

Then one day the phone rang. I jumped on it, thinking maybe it was Vivi, calling to explain herself to me. I answered almost immediately. Nothing. There was no reply. Just silence. Then I heard footsteps behind me, someone running across the hall. I hung up and went to explore the flat. It was as empty as ever. The window was open, releasing a cool chill around the rooms.

I shut it and went back to work. I told myself that things like that happened all the time, I'd forget to shut windows a lot, and occasionally next door's cat would wander in. Just coincidences.

The next day the same thing happened. The phone rang and I picked it up, said 'hello' and there was still no answer. Just the hum of the line and that was it. Then the footsteps behind me, again I moved towards the sound and there was nothing there. It was disconcerting. So I had a stiff drink, to snap myself out of it.

This happened once or twice a week from then on. Always the silent phone call and then the footsteps. If the window was open or shut it didn't matter. This was not a cat. This was something else. I dialled 1471 once. The woman's voice on the other end told me that the number could not be reached. It didn't even exist. I could barely sleep. I saw her every time I closed my eyes and every time I dropped off she was there in that same dream.

I became afraid of the phone ringing. I was so confused. I wanted everything to stop. I'd seen her again a day or so before, on one of my few trips out of the flat. I'd gone for a walk and then got on the tube, just surrounded myself with people to try and take my mind off all these things that had been going on, things that I couldn't explain – but she was there, on the train. I could've sworn it was her, so I went up to her and tapped her on the shoulder, my heart in my stomach.

She turned around and looked straight at me – it wasn't her at all. It was like a scene from a dodgy film where the main guy is looking for someone and you think he's found them but it's a random stranger. I just apologised. It was a walking horror story.

It was getting worse. She was invading my life every day. Wherever I went she would be there. I'd catch a glimpse and I'd turn to look and she'd be gone. She was always wearing that red dress, always so beautiful. I wasn't even mad at her anymore. Not by this point. I was just scared.

My reasoning was that if she was back in London I might see her once or twice a year but she'd have told me. She wouldn't stalk me and there wouldn't be those phone calls. I wouldn't hear her when I was alone.

I'd been avoiding mentioning it to anyone. When it started I spoke to friends about it, they laughed and told me to man up and deal with it. When I mentioned it again a few weeks later they got really angry at me, they told me to stop whining about *some stupid French chick* and learn how to have some fun.

So I let a few months pass by before saying anything to anyone about it. I wanted to hide it but I needed to talk to someone and this group of people was all I really had left. They thought it was over, since I never spoke about it. When I told my best friend Dean about everything that had happened, he looked at me like I was crazy, but I could see he was genuinely concerned. He said he hadn't seen or heard from her, nobody had. She was gone. He knew that I'd been drinking too much. He tried to make me talk to someone. A professional, he said, because this was serious.

I started trawling the internet for people who'd experienced stuff like this. I'd sit at my desk, bottle of whisky at my fingertips. All I found was a bunch of lonely people who were still madly in love with their ex-partners and kept dreaming about them or seeing them because they miss them, or want them back. I thought maybe I fell into that category too, but then the phone calls became more frequent and when I picked up, the line was not quite as silent as before. Now I could hear a crackling, and a high-pitched hissing sound. I'd just hang up and tell myself it was nothing and drink myself to sleep and then wake up in a cold sweat from that same dream.

I became a recluse, not wanting to see her again out in the street. I was a wreck. I was convinced that it was her because I'd started to hear her voice behind the crackling noise on the phone line. But she was like a ghost. I couldn't contact her at all, not by myself anyway.

So, I found out where her mum lived in France. I made up my mind to call her. I thought maybe she'd be able to make her stop calling. My French was always a little rusty but I'd rehearsed what to say and told myself that everything would be ok. I wasn't sure if she even knew who I was, but I thought maybe Vivienne might have mentioned me. She was the love of my life, after all.

I had this speech all prepared and written down:

Bonjour Madame Caron,
Mon nom est James, à Londres. Je m'excuse pour mon
Français. Il n'est pas très bon. J'étais copain Vivienne
alors qu'elle était ici l'an dernier. Pouvez-vous s'il vous
plaît lui dire d'arrêter de me contacter. Je l'aime, et
ses appels téléphoniques constants font ma vie très
difficile. J'espère que vous comprenez. Je suis désolé
de vous déranger à cette question, mais je ne peux
pas passer d'elle. Vous connaissez à Londres où elle
séjourne?
Merci Madame.

I was asking her to tell Vivi to stop calling me because it was making it difficult for me to get over her leaving and to ask if she knew where Vivi was staying in London. It was polite and succinct. I'd hoped she would understand.

The response I got was most definitely not what I had expected and sent a chill down my spine. I will never forget what she said.

She said, in English, so I could fully understand, 'Why do you say these things to me? My daughter has been in a coma for six months.'

She sounded distraught and I didn't want to press the issue further, but it just didn't make any sense. I needed to know. I took a second to catch my breath and asked what happened. She said that a few days after she reached France she was in an accident and one of the cars caught fire. She had been in hospital since...

I went to visit her in France. The hospital garden was filled with white blossom trees, the petals falling like snow in the breeze.

I walked into her room and pulled back the curtain. Vivienne was in a coma, still breathing and still beautiful. I could see the white petals from her window.

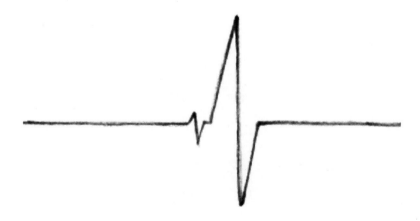

Lost Soul

Lulu Badger

He is panting as he lifts the latch on the door to the inn, pushes it open and stumbles through. He leans his back on the door, pushes heavily against the wind and the rain and forces it closed. The latch drops and all is calm. Standing there, dripping on the mat, he is struck by a wave of heat, overwhelming by its contrast to the cold outside.

From behind the bar on the far side of the room, a man with grey hair, blue eyes and a kindly face welcomes him in. He smiles at the visitor as if he were a long-lost friend. It is a welcoming smile, offering solace and comfort.

'Good afternoon, sir,' says the barman.

'Do you have a telephone I can use?'

'I'm afraid not, sir. The lines are being worked on. We had a letter.'

'What about a mobile?'

'I'm afraid not, sir. Is there something wrong?'

'I lost my backpack over the cliff,' says the visitor. 'Slipped over on the path. Gone.'

He rests his back against the door as he speaks, disorientation and faintness making his legs weak. Looking up and around the room, he takes in the brightness and heat of the fire to his right, the black and white pictures of unknown faces and places looking down at him from the oak-panelled wall above, the two deep leather armchairs on either side and, ahead of him, the bar, with its array of bottles and glasses.

Although it feels familiar to him, he can't recall being here before. He is aware of an overall numbness, a cold so deep in his bones that he is past the pain of it. As the heat begins to seep into him, he starts to shiver. He puts his hands out in front of him. They emerge from his sodden sleeves and he studies them. White and shaking, he feels that they are coming back to life, tingling at first then cramped and painful. He puts them into his pockets as the barman speaks.

'That's dreadful, sir. These paths are treacherous in the rain, aren't they?' He is wiping glasses with a dishcloth. 'Were you hurt?'

The visitor has to think. He isn't aware of any sprains or strains. Just the pain of warming. He looks to the floor again. He is trying to gather his thoughts. Just two seconds ago his predicament had been quite clear: his hurried escape, the rain, the slip, the fall, the loss.

Now, as he stands on the mat, disoriented and weak-kneed with shock, he tries to picture the events on the cliff. He tries to focus on what has happened as if he is recalling a dream but, with every effort, his memory becomes weaker. There, in the shadowy world of half-remembered dreams, he sees the path and feels his feet slipping beneath him. He is afraid of falling. The sea is crashing on the rocks beneath him. Gorse rips at his coat from one side and an impenetrable wall of grey on the other blocks the horizon from view.

'I slipped. Well, I think I…slipped and then…it fell and was…it was gone…' says the man, searching his memory.

'I'm so glad you found your way here,' says the barman kindly. 'The letter said that everything would be done by four. That's only an hour or so. Perhaps you could wait?'

The rain is lashing at the windows and the trees outside are bending in the wind. A growing sense of uneasiness sweeps over the visitor. Something tells him that he should not be here, that he was on his way somewhere else. Standing on the threshold to this place, with dripping jacket, mud-covered boots and a storm raging outside, he feels sure of some imminent danger, but he has no idea whether it is behind him or in front of him.

Lifting his head, he searches the room for something familiar, somewhere to anchor and shelter from the storm. His eyes settle on the armchairs sitting sentinel beside the fire. Deep brown leather whispers comfort, inviting him to take his place and soak up the warmth that spills out from the flames. Succumbing to the temptation of their embrace and comforted by the geniality of the grey-haired man, he finds himself removing his coat and saying, 'Yes. I could wait.'

No sooner have these words passed his lips, than he finds himself in the arms of the worn leather, a soft, velvet cushion at his back. His coat hangs on a peg above the fireplace.

He does not remember sitting. The chairs had called, but when had he answered? When did he walk across the room? He had been on the mat, the rain and wind behind him, his jacket dripping. He had been cold. His eyes had found the chairs, so warm, so inviting, and now, here he is, sitting by the fire.

It's as if his very thoughts have transported him from there to here. And his coat? Did he hang it there or was it the barman?

It doesn't really matter. He is warm and safe as he watches steam rising from the soaked jacket. White wisps rise and disappear into the ether. Something becoming nothing. He is a wisp of white. His thoughts are clouds of steam.

'Would you like a drink, sir?' the barman asks.

'A drink? Yes...a drink would be good.'

He watches as the pint is pulled. Gold liquid fills the glass as the barman extols the virtues of that particular brew. The man licks his lips as he waits. Then the glass is in his hand and he is sipping his first sip. It tastes good. He closes his eyes to savour the malty liquid. He doesn't think he has ever tried an ale so delicious. It tastes wholesome, satisfying and healing. Like a panacea, it calms and comforts him.

When he opens his eyes he finds to his relief that, for a moment, he has become an ordinary man sheltering from the rain in a warm and cosy pub. He smiles to himself as the beer and flames warm his very core.

'Walking holiday, sir?' says the barman.

The question pulls him back into focus. The nebulous world

he and his glass have occupied retreats rapidly and anxiety creeps in to take its place. Glimpsing himself in a far corner of his mind, he sees fear, hears the pounding of feet, the gasping for breath, a woman, his own laughter.

Reality? Memories? Dreams? He doesn't know which. They are disconnected pictures moving across a screen telling stories of another time. Whatever they are, they speak of danger.

He must hide them from the barman. No one must know his mind. He does not know it himself.

'Yes,' he answers. 'Of sorts.'

The barman smiles and returns to his task of wiping glasses, carefully placing them back on the shelf. The clock on the mantelpiece ticks.

Looking into the fire, the visitor is lost in his thoughts. But they are not the right ones. He is running from an unknown enemy towards loss and darkness. Seeking solace in his pint and drinking deeply, he forces himself to return to the present. It is working. The drugs of heat, ale and comfort engulf him again and bad memory is waning. Flames lick around logs and whisper pretty secrets. They curl and dance over the wood while the wood squeals in delight.

'It's very warm in here,' he says.

'We like to keep it warm, sir.'

'It's quiet too. Is it always this quiet?'

'Not really, sir. You need to take advantage of this. It will all change shortly,' says the barman, cloth in hand.

Aware that this comment should prompt further questioning, the visitor cannot find the energy to do so. With each sip of ale, he feels himself relax further. He simply doesn't care what is coming. Or is it that he is losing his sanity?

His troubles, if he ever had any, are disappearing like the moisture from his coat, leaving nothing but a vague memory of what was before. All he can see and feel is here, now, in this place and surrounded by these secure walls. He watches the clock as its hands tick rhythmically around its face.

'My grandmother had wallpaper like that in her front room,' he says, looking at the red flock behind the timepiece.

'Yes. It was very popular at one time, I believe.'

The man shuffles forward in his chair, eager to speak.

'My grandmother died when I was twelve. It was the first funeral I went to. We waited in her front room for the cortege. We had to keep really quiet. We waited for hours in that room. Everyone was whispering and wearing black. I couldn't look at their faces so I just stared at the wall. I suppose that's why I remember that wallpaper so well.'

The fire crackles and hisses in front of him.

After a few seconds more he adds, 'I don't remember crying.'

'I'm sure there are many things we don't remember, sir. Don't you think?' observes the barman.

'So many things we don't remember,' echoes the man as he sits back in his chair and gazes into the flames.

'And, yet, so many that we do.'

'Yes. So many that we do.'

'Like the wallpaper, sir. Sometimes all we need is a little nudge to help us remember these 'forgotten' things.'

The visitor seems not to hear him. He is entranced by the fire, watching as images of his life are played out in the flames. Pictures of people and places, voices and visits. His mother pulling him back from the kerb, his brother locking him in the garden shed, his father shouting. There's his grandma! A big bowl of sweets in her lap, inviting him to help himself. And there's grandpa teaching him how to fish in the old canal. Himself, riding his brand new bicycle, all shiny and yellow. He loved that bike!

And then, as quickly as they came, the images fade, changing back into flames. The noises of his childhood revert to snaps and cracks as wood is transformed into ash and smoke.

He feels cheated. There is so much more he would like to have seen, so many other people he would like to have remembered, so many forgotten things still invisible. He wanted to see his mother again, even for an instant. Searching for her in the flames, his eyes dampen a little.

'Are you all right, sir?' the barman asks. 'You seem a little confused.'

'Fine, thank you,' lies the visitor, clearing his throat. 'It's just the fire. It's so... I was watching the flames.' He looks up at the barman hoping to find some reassurance in his kindly face.

'Watch away, sir!' the barman says and, as he does so, the fire seems to regenerate from within, the flames circling and climbing, the wood swelling, the heat rising.

His face burning, the visitor tries to pull back from the fireplace, but finds himself unable to do so. Every effort he makes to push the chair further from the heat is fruitless. He is unable to move his legs. Unable to shift his position. And yet, drawn towards the source of his discomfort.

'Hey!' he says, alarm rising within him. 'What the hell...?'

'Relax,' says the barman. 'It really is an excellent fire.'

The flames take form once more. He sees himself at school with another boy. He has the boy pinned against a wall. The boy is crying but he doesn't let go. Now he is driving, a pretty girl laughing beside him. He drives faster and faster until she stops laughing and begs him to stop. He doesn't. His wedding day. The church is full of hats and buttons. She is at home with the baby. She is crying. Now he is shaking hands with a man in a suit. His first deal!

Cars and faceless women spin by as he looks on. Now he is standing over a woman's body, her lifeless eyes so familiar yet so despised. Then his son, a grown man, stands alone on the grass, looking into a hole in the ground. Himself again, tangled between sheets in a hotel room...

'Please,' he says. 'Tell me what's going on.'

The barman smiles. Yet, somehow, it is not the same smile as before. What had been a kindly, warm expression now has a hint of malevolence. A look of self-satisfaction comes into the barman's eyes and the corners of his mouth become deliberately set, held by some inner thought rather than in natural response to his companion.

'Is the fire bothering you, sir?'

'Who are you?' asks the visitor, as fear and confusion overcome him once more. 'Where am I?'

'I think you dozed off, sir.'

'No, I didn't! I was looking at the fire and then...then I saw things...it was real. I don't want to see any more. Let me out of this chair. I want to leave now.'

'Leave? It is not time to leave yet, sir. I haven't called last orders!' The barman laughs to himself.

The distant sound of sirens drowns out the laughter. There is a flash of blue through the glass and a wail as a screaming car speeds by.

'Another poor soul gone over the cliff,' observes the barman.

'Stop them! I need to get out of here!' calls the visitor.

But they do not stop and the sirens and lights fade and disappear. The silence that follows is absolute. There is no clock, no crackle, no rain beating on the window. A chill comes over him and all is quiet.

'It was me, wasn't it?' he asks.

'Yes, sir. It was you.'

'So I am...'

'Dead sir? Oh yes! You are most certainly dead!' He laughs again.

'Who are you?' he asks again, panic rising.

The barman comes around behind his visitor, puts his hand on his shoulder, leans down and says, quietly, 'The fire has shown you who you are, sir. From that, can you not discern *my* identity?'

Looking out of the window, the visitor can see that the rain has stopped. The light has completely faded and there is only darkness beyond the glass.

He looks towards the door expecting to see its thick oak panels and cast iron latch but instead he sees only darkness. The deepest black imaginable fills the shape of the door frame, as if it is the entrance to a deep mine, heading downwards for eternity to a place where light has never reached.

He is drawn towards it. Something magnetic is calling him and he has to hold the arms of the chair to stop himself from falling.

The barman comes around to face him, his eyes burning.

'Welcome to Hell.'

The Inheritance

Danielle Charles

My tale begins and ends with an old cottage, grey stone and derelict, standing lonely and stark against the high moorland that rises up behind it. There is an overgrown apple orchard and a wood by a stream. It is the cottage that belonged to an old farmer: my father. The cottage that, for a time, belonged to me.

When we came up to Yorkshire that autumn of 1939, my father had been dead for ten years. His death was nothing of note: old age and a weakened heart, fingernails that turned blue and a chest filled up with fluid. He was the fifth generation of Dolbys to live and die in that place, raising sheep and pigs, scraping by in a hard and solitary life. Loneliness was the currency of his days.

All that I knew of my history then was that my mother had gone mad towards the end of her pregnancy with me. Two weeks before I was due, she disappeared. No one knew where and no one ever saw her again. The next thing anyone heard was when my swaddled form was discovered abandoned on a bus stop bench in Bradford. By then, my father didn't want anything to do with me. He couldn't stand the sight of me, said I reminded him of the disgrace of my mother. So from there on, my life began anew. The only memories I had were the vague images that occasionally haunted my dreams, slipping into hazy obscurity whenever I woke.

I grew up in Whitechapel. The story of how I came to be there is a long one, so I will say only that I was fortunate. The family who took me in were poor, working-class people – but they were kind. And they did their best to make me feel like one of their own.

It was in Whitechapel that I met my husband James. In Whitechapel where we began to dream of a better life for ourselves, for the child I was carrying in my belly: a life of fresh, open air with an apple orchard, a grey stone cottage and a wood by a stream. It was the promise of *some day* that tormented and encouraged us both, that we would say to each other like a prayer. James coming in, weary, clinking a few quid into the jar. *Some day.* Me, washing the laundry till my fingers cracked and split and ached to the bone. *Some day.*

And then I received the letter, addressed from a solicitor in York. The letter telling me that they had found a will. And I was to inherit everything: the cottage, fifteen acres of boggy, moorland pasture and a few hundred quid. It wasn't much. But to James and I, it was all we could have asked for.

On the train to York, I read over the will again, the words of it worn into my mind like footprints on a muddy track. I was searching for meaning in the roughness of the paper, in the spaces between the letters, in the rhythm of the words. But there was simply no sense to it. To why this man – who never once tried to contact me when he was alive – should decide to give me all his belongings when he was dead. Or why he should state as a condition of the inheritance that I was to be *with child*. I had thought it only a strange coincidence, a stroke of luck that I was five months along when the letter came.

We arrived in York just after one o'clock and took the bus to Denholme. It only went as far as the village centre, so from there we had to walk the remaining two miles up the lonely and twisting path climbing the dale. The wind tugged at our clothes and pushed us along impatiently, as if it were trying to hurry us out of its way.

And then, there it was.

Though the apple orchard was badly overgrown, though the house looked abandoned and forlorn, it was the one: the place that was in our dreams, in our visions. It was the very house, down to the moss-covered stones. The stark and wild moor stretched up behind it, cupping the house in its hands like a precious jewel.

Mr Barnaby, the solicitor, was already there, waiting. He was sweating profusely and pulling at his collar, which he seemed to suspect of choking him.

We shook hands and Mr Barnaby motioned us towards the cottage.

'You go on inside and have a look round,' he said, wiping the sweat from his palms onto the fabric of his trousers. 'I'll wait for your friend to catch up so he doesn't miss us.'

'What friend, Mr Barnaby?' I asked, turning to look behind me.

'The man who was walking up t'lane with you just now,' he said. 'The man in the red jacket.'

James and I exchanged a wary look.

'If there was a man,' said James, studying Mr Barnaby, 'I can tell you he was not with us.'

Mr Barnaby struggled for several minutes before he finally managed to unlock the heavy front door. It swung open of its own inertia, creaking at the hinges and then we walked inside.

The light was dim, the air dusty and stale, smelling of wet stone and of damp shadowy places. The faded wallpaper was falling away in strips. Many of the beams in the ceiling were badly rotted and there were gaping holes in the roof where the rotten boards had collapsed and dusty beams of sunlight pooled through. A house martin swooped above our heads, her chicks peering out from a nest tucked up under one of the rafters with open, expectant mouths.

When I walked through those musty rooms that day, I had such a curious feeling, as if I had each foot settled into a different world. On one hand, I was seeing a life unfold before me – a life I wanted, a life I had dreamed of. On the other – a life behind. One as wonderful as the other seemed horrible and I wasn't sure which emotion should take precedence: whether I should feel sublime joy or a terrible loathing. And yet, the past was the past, I told myself, looking out of the top window over the orchard, the sun smouldering into the horizon in a pale orange glow.

Mr Barnaby looked surprised when James told him we wished to keep it. He had, as I recall, suggested that perhaps we think it over for a night. Be absolutely certain. We could find a smaller property in better repair with the money, he'd said. Of course, I thought it only had to do with the state of the place, that he thought we were mad to want to live in that house, forlorn and surrounded as it was by the gusting winds of the moor. And I thought the same again when I signed the papers and Mr Barnaby had smiled at me apologetically – a smile as if he had a rotten turnip under his tongue and was trying to conceal it from me. Though I would be lying if I said I didn't sense something then.

We started on repairs. James replaced the rotted beams and began the process of putting on a new roof. I set to work on the years of grime that had collected over everything. It was hard work and slow going. But I enjoyed it: the cadence of it. There was a sense that with every wall scrubbed, every window pane cleaned, I was excavating something wonderful, bringing the house back to life. And I fancied, as I worked, that the house was in some way grateful to me.

We rented a small room in town until the cottage was fit for habitation. As we came and went from the dale, people seemed

wary of us, stopping on the street to turn and look as we passed, as if we had just stepped out of the stonework on the church or climbed up out of a puddle. I assumed this was the way people were in small villages. Especially in the north where people are naturally colder in temperament, like the weather. Anything beyond that I attributed to the story I was sure people knew, of my abandonment on a Bradford bench. To them, I thought, I was like someone from a myth. I was forcing them to remember a past that was, in their eyes, best forgotten.

We had been there nearly three weeks when James suggested we should venture into The George, the local pub whose candlelit windows and murmur of voices seemed welcoming as we passed it by in the sharp October air.

'We can't hide forever,' he called back, making his way ahead of me down the twisting, windswept path leading back to town from the house. 'If we're going to live here, we need to be a part of things. Not like him, wasting away up there all on his own. We have to make an effort.'

Of course I could see the sense of it, but I had such apprehension. Not just that people would turn and stare, that they would whisper behind their hands and I would feel as unwelcome as a fox in a hen-house. I expected that and I could endure it. But rather, it was that these people had known my mother, my father. They knew things about them: things I was almost certain I did not wish to know.

The reaction as we pushed through the door was not at all what I anticipated. Not a single person turned their heads. There was no lull in the drone of conversation. Not a single motion out of place. But the atmosphere physically stiffened, as though the entire room were geared towards the one collective purpose of ignoring us. In some ways, I thought that was almost worse.

The publican beamed at us, as if we were nothing more

than a couple of tourists: a bit of entertainment and extra brass for his pockets. I stood and took the room in as James put in our order. There were faded armchairs pushed up towards the fire, cigarette burns on the leather backs of the pub stools. The walls and ceilings were stained yellow with nicotine. And then, I felt a rough hand clasp mine, calloused and weathered, the veins on the back like the purple worms hanging out of a thrush's mouth.

I looked up to find an old whiskered man, his sallow cheeks caving in from lack of teeth. His eyes clouded over in a milky film. There was something in his face that made me turn away, fixing my gaze instead on the worn wooden handles of the taps and the glint of light off the pint glasses stacked behind the bar.

'John Dolby's girl,' he said, tightening his clasp, his hands dry and cold.

Though he was old, his grip was tight, and I couldn't pull my hand free. I stared at the back of James' head, willing the tweed cap to turn around to rescue me.

The man slapped his tongue against the roof of his mouth, the sound dry and raspy.

'Yes,' he said, both of us staring ahead, as if he weren't actually talking to me at all. 'You've made your way, haven't you? And now,' he said, squeezing my fingers together, almost painfully, 'I'd make your way back. If you know what's good for you, lass.'

And with that, he dropped my hand and ambled towards the bar, not once looking back. The murmur of conversations went on as before. The flickering of candle flames, the crack of the fire. But I had a sense, somehow, that everyone had heard, that the entire room had shared his sentiments.

I just couldn't bring myself to tell James. He seemed so happy as we walked back to our room, rubbing his hands together in the cold night air and babbling on like a school boy. He had spent most of the night talking to the publican and a few of the farm lads, laughing and throwing darts.

'Did you know,' he asked, as we were dressing for bed, 'that your family – the Dolbys that is – have lived up on that moor since the sixteenth century?'

'No,' I said, 'I did not.'

'They've been there so long,' he went on, seated on the edge of the bed, pulling off his socks, 'there's even a local myth about them. Apparently, the entire moor used to belong to a faerie. A Sidhe prince, *The Man in the Red Jacket* they call him.'

He leaned over, reaching for his pyjama top from the side table. 'When the Dolbys first came to the moor, they made a pact with this spirit, this – whatever you want to call it – that in exchange for the right of the family to live there, each new generation would offer their...their...'

James stopped, scratching his head, 'You know it's the damnedest thing, my love, but I simply can't remember.'

He sat for a moment, staring intently at the wall then resumed the unbuttoning of his shirt. 'Ah well, it's all a bunch of stuff and nonsense anyway.'

It was only later, as I lay there listening to the tide of James' breath in the darkness, that I remembered what Mr Barnaby had said. The man who was walking up t'lane with you. The man with the red jacket.

It was a good month after that when we finally moved into the cottage. I was nearly eight months along then, so we had been rushing to get things ready. I was overcome with the strong desire that my child should be born in that cottage – the place where I should have been rightly born myself. I believed that somehow, I could dissolve the past with the prospect of the future. Cancel out what had happened to me.

That first night, we slept on a mattress laid out before the fireplace in the main room. We hadn't fully cleared the chimney yet, so the fire smoked terribly, and we fell asleep with our throats and eyes raw from the harshness of the air.

So I thought, next morning, that the smoke was the cause of the dreams. Dreams where I was running over the moor, my legs sinking into the cold boggy ground, stuck down to the knee. Terrified to turn round and see what was pursuing me. Terrified of the putrid blackness spread out before me.

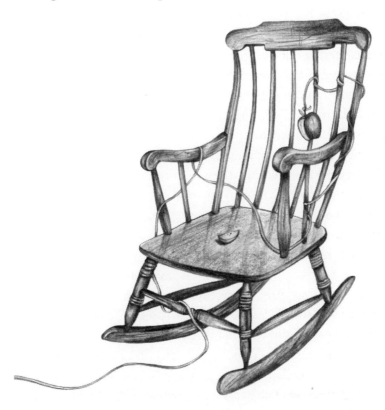

But the dream occurred again the next night. And again the night after. And the night after that. So that all the nights of December passed me by in a surreal haze of terror: the terror that is all the greater because it cannot be defined. It cannot be named. But when I woke, I would feel my baby moving within me, a dance of tendons and joints, of tiny hands and footsteps. And I would be comforted, until the night came again.

And then, mid-January – just seven days before my due date, I had a different dream.

In this dream, I was seated in the corner of the cottage in an old rocking chair. My baby was nursing in my arms and there was nothing but the sound of the chair, creaking as it rocked, back and forth, back and forth. So that I was nearly lulled into a daze, staring out into the darkness. I remember remarking to myself, even in my dream, how very bright the stars seemed out the window. As though they were much closer than normal and I could've reached out and plucked one down from the sky like an apple if I had wished.

Then a knock came at the door, loud and resonant, as if it had come from within the very fibres of the wood itself. I hitched the baby against my hip and got up. The rocking chair still creaked behind me, back and forth, back and forth. The knocking had grown louder, more insistent, so that when at last I reached it, the sound was nearly deafening, reverberating in my very bones, amplifying within my skull. I wanted to put my hands to my ears, to scream – anything to make it stop. But when I looked down, my little babe slept on, her eyelids twitching peacefully with her dreams.

I placed my hand on the handle of the door and then immediately recoiled. The flesh of my fingers singed red where they had touched. The brass was glowing with a radiant indigo light, like the indefinable blue in the deepest incarnations of a flame. And the stench: putrid and sour, as if a decaying corpse was laid out in the room with me. It was not until I looked down, and saw the maroon blood pooling on the floor under my skirts, felt it trickling down the inside of my thigh, warm and sticky as honey, that I realized the smell was coming from me. From my own blood.

The handle of the door was rattling now. The scent was so sharp in my nostrils that I wanted to retch. But still, I willed myself towards the window, struggling away from the door as if moving against the flow of a river. And when at last I grasped the edge of the sill with my fingers, I could just glimpse him in the faint light from the stars. The man in the red jacket, carrying my baby in his arms towards the darkness of the moor. The baby in my own arms, gone.

'I've remembered,' James said, the following day, 'What it was the Dolbys promised.'

But by then, there was no need to tell me. The signs of life within me had already stopped.

Shadow Play

Colin Bradbury

'You're going to love it,' Tommy says as the car negotiates another of the hairpin bends coiled around the hillside. 'Look at that view!'

'I've already seen enough rice paddies to last a lifetime,' Nina laughs. 'How do they manage to squeeze those little fields onto steep hills like that?' She points to the rice terraces carved into the rising ground. Each terrace is bordered by an earthen wall that stops the water in the rice paddies from spilling down the hillside: a landscape of living contour lines.

'Because this is Bali,' Tommy replies, 'people will plant rice on any spare bit of land. Rice is a religion here.'

The car rounds a final bend and low wooden buildings appear ahead. Passing a sign with the words *Welcome to Ubud International Resort*, the car pulls up in front of the hotel. A man in a traditional, riotously patterned batik shirt is standing there, waiting.

'Welcome back, boss!' he says, smiling broadly.

'I told you, Rizal, don't call me *boss*,' Tommy says, frowning in mock annoyance, 'and where on earth did you get that shirt?'

'Just trying to brighten the place up, boss,' he grins. Nina has stepped out of the car and comes around to join them.

'Nina, this old rogue is Rizal, hotel manager. Rizal, this is my wife, Nina. I thought it was about time she came along on one of these trips, learn it's not all cocktails around the pool.'

After dropping the luggage at their villa, Rizal invites them for cocktails by the swimming pool. Nina will never let me forget this, he thinks. Around the edge, well-heeled European, American and Japanese families sprawl on sun loungers, their impeccably behaved children playing in the shallow end. Tommy sips his cocktail and turns to Rizal.

'So how's it all coming on?' he asks.

Tommy has been sent from London to check on the hotel's

new project: a spa facility being built on land next to the resort. A cloud passes over Rizal's face and he hesitates before replying.

'I can't say all the villagers are happy about it. I'm sure they'll come around eventually.'

'I don't understand,' says Tommy. 'We paid a fair price for the land, didn't we?'

'More than fair,' Rizal says. 'But that's not the problem.'

'What is it then?'

'You're quarter Balinese, Tommy. Can't you guess?'

Tommy's grandmother had come from the island, moving to London at the turn of the 20th century with her English plantation manager husband. Tommy's Indonesian heritage was the reason the company had asked him to oversee this project, though he felt almost as much of a foreigner here as Nina.

'Of course, it's the rice, isn't it?' he says.

Rizal nods but Nina looks puzzled.

'The rice – what do you mean?'

'The Balinese are very attached to their rice fields, Nina,' Rizal explains.

'Yes,' she says. 'We were talking about it in the car.'

Tommy cuts in.

'But if we paid a fair price, why aren't the villagers happy?'

Rizal sighs.

'The fields were owned by an old man who rented them out to several other families to grow rice on. When he sold to us, they lost their livelihoods. But it wasn't just that.'

'Well, what was it then?' Tommy persists.

'The fields are sacred to the villagers. They felt betrayed when the old man sold them.'

'Oh come on – sacred rice paddies?' Nina says. 'How hokey is that? Tommy's always telling me that Indonesia's a modern country now.'

Rizal looks suddenly serious.

'Modern? In Jakarta and some other parts of Java, sure. Maybe even in the resorts down on the coast of Bali where the old ways have been buried under all the development. But here in the hill villages, you don't have to dig far below the surface to find the old Indonesia. Here, people still hold onto their beliefs.'

'People?' says Nina. 'What about you – do you go for all this stuff?'

Tommy interrupts.

'That's a bit harsh, Nina.'

'That's OK,' Rizal says. 'Look, I've spent lots of time in Europe and America. I can understand that in a big city, all this stuff looks like a lot of superstitious nonsense. But I was brought up here in the hills and I can tell you that I've seen and heard things that I can't explain. At least, not in a way that anybody outside Bali would understand.'

'I still think the villagers were just jealous that the old man got rich from selling his fields,' Tommy says, shaking his head.

'That's what the police thought when they investigated his disappearance.'

'Disappearance?' says Nina.

'According to his wife, he saw someone in the rice paddies one night and went to investigate: he never came back. The police couldn't find any evidence of foul play, especially since there was no body and the money the old man had got for the land was untouched. He just disappeared.'

'Do you think one of the men from the village did away with him – you know, revenge?' Tommy asks.

'No. Because the last thing the old man said before he disappeared was that the figure in the paddy fields was a woman.'

Later that evening, Tommy and Nina are walking back to the main hotel buildings from their villa. The sun has gone down but the air is still heavy with humidity, even up here in the mountains. The cicadas have started their evening chorus in the banyan trees lining the path.

'Strange about the old man disappearing like that,' Nina says.

'I'm sure there's a rational explanation,' Tommy replies. 'Anyway, let's forget about all that and just enjoy dinner. By the way, Rizal told me there's a *Wayang* performance in the local village later on. We should go – it'd be a good way of showing the villagers that we're sensitive to local customs. Good PR never goes amiss.'

'*Wayang* – what on earth is that?' asks Nina.

'The most ancient form of entertainment in Indonesia: a kind of shadow theatre,' Tommy explains. '*Wayang kulit* – it means 'ghost puppets'. They hang a big white sheet and shine a light from behind. The flat puppets cast a shadow on the sheet, and that's what the audience sees. It's all about light and shadow, good and evil. And there's always a *gamelan* orchestra.'

'Help me out,' she says, smiling.

'*Gamelan*,' he repeats. 'The musicians hit thick metal bars with small hammers – a bit like a xylophone I suppose – and there are other instruments. Little gongs and things. It's a weird sound, but very atmospheric.'

'Sounds thrilling,' she says, arching an eyebrow, 'but I think I'll leave the PR to you. I feel serious jet-lag coming on.'

Tommy shrugs. 'I admit, it doesn't sound very exciting when I try to describe it. But when I was a boy, my grandmother had some old records of *gamelan* music she used to play for me. Sitting in her little house in London, I'd close my eyes and it seemed like it came from another world. I guess to her it just sounded like home.'

After dinner, Tommy walks Nina to the villa and then turns back down the path towards the hotel where Rizal will be waiting with a jeep for their trip to the village. The path is only

dimly lit and the banyan trees take on strange forms in the half light. Tommy is suddenly aware of a figure on the path ahead of him, but a moment later the curve of the path obscures his view. When the path straightens again, the figure is closer. It's a woman: another guest or a member of staff, he guesses. But something about her dress and the way she carries herself makes him unsure.

She stops at a place where the path passes close to the edge of the hotel grounds by the rice fields. In the glow of the lights he sees that she is young, in her twenties probably, and is wearing traditional Balinese dress of green and gold. He can't see her face, but notices what looks like a plant in her left hand. Something about her seems to be of another time. She turns off the path and heads towards the rice fields. Tommy finds himself overwhelmed with a desire to follow her, to find out who she is. But Rizal's voice breaks the silence.

'Hey boss, I was coming to look for you. We need to get going.'

Tommy turns in the direction of Rizal's voice, and when he looks back he sees, with an unexpected pang of regret, that the woman has gone.

As they walk to the hotel, he asks Rizal about the woman. With her traditional garb, she must work at the hotel, surely? Rizal's mouth tightens for a moment and then he questions Tommy closely about how the woman looked, what exactly she was wearing, whether she spoke. At first, he assumes that Rizal is just trying to work out which one of the hotel staff it might be, but the intensity of his questions leaves an uneasy feeling.

They are bumping down the road in the jeep, Rizal at the wheel. The modern infrastructure around the hotel melts away and suddenly they are deep in old Bali. A few minutes later, they pull into the square.

A crowd is gathering in front of a makeshift stage with a wooden structure on top. A tattered sheet hangs from a long board. Tommy and Rizal sit down on the dusty floor as the performance starts, two large oil lamps backlighting the puppets. The lamplight is not steady, like an electric light, but uneven and elemental, flickering and flaring to its own rhythm. There are no other lights around the square and the audience is hidden, the only light coming from the show itself.

Then the *gamelan* orchestra starts up, quietly at first and then building, the metallic sound of the hammers on the iron keys creating a hypnotic wall of noise. Tommy is engulfed by a sound that has something unknowable and ancient about it, the past reaching into the present, demanding to be heard. The first ghost puppets appear, their flat figures casting flickering shadows onto the cloth screen, moving in and out of the audience's vision, like spirits.

Before long, Tommy realises with growing unease that the story is about a dispute over some rice fields. Puppets representing evil spirits are trying to take them from the villagers. Even in the dark, Tommy feels the eyes of the villagers on him and his stomach tightens. Have they brought him here to take revenge on the hotel for desecrating their land? The *gamelan* orchestra's playing reaches a frenetic peak and Tommy imagines his name being whispered over and over in the jumbled chaos of the music.

Suddenly the music stops. The oil lamps are covered and the darkness deepens, profound and impenetrable. When the lights come back on, a new puppet is in the midst of the others: a woman. Astonished, Tommy recognises it as the girl in the grounds of the hotel. He watches the climax of the show, transfixed: a battle between the evil spirits and the woman, a goddess of some kind. As the orchestra resumes, this time in an insistent sonic assault, the puppets dart back and forth across the stage, the flickering light adding to the confusion and chaos.

Eventually, the goddess and her army are the only ones left. The evil spirits have been vanquished and the fields saved.

Then it's over. Oil lamps are lit and the spell broken as the crowd melts away. Tommy regards them apprehensively, but they pay him no heed. Maybe his imagination had been playing tricks on him. Tommy and Rizal stand up and stretch their limbs as the puppeteers begin to dismantle the stage, under the direction of an older man whose quiet authority marks him out as the leader. There is an infinite care about the way that they lay the puppets in their boxes, as if they are living, breathing beings.

'Who is he?' Tommy asks.

'The puppet master,' Rizal replies. 'A very important man in the village.'

'I must speak to him,' Tommy tells Rizal. 'I need to ask him something.'

Rizal nods, but without much enthusiasm, Tommy can't help noticing. They pick their way through the departing crowd. As they draw close to him, Tommy sees that the puppet master's face is furrowed with deep lines, like the rice terraces themselves. Tommy can't hide his surprise when the puppet master addresses him in English.

'I perform the *Wayang* for foreigners for many years. And I know who you are. What do you want from me?'

'The puppet who appeared at the end, the woman – who was she?'

The old man's face hardens.

'Yes, you have seen her before,' he says.

Tommy is confused.

'How do you...? Who is she?'

'*Dewi Sri*, goddess of rice. She protects the rice fields from our enemies.'

From deep inside one of the boxes containing the puppets,

he produces a tattered book. He opens it and hands it to Tommy.

'Here is a picture.'

For a moment, Tommy stops breathing. The picture shows a young woman with downcast eyes, dressed in green and gold. In her hand she holds a rice plant.

The puppet master continues.

'But you know this already.'

'Why would I know?' Tommy asks.

The old man smiles again.

'Because the mother of your mother is from Bali, is she not? You must know that *Dewi Sri* will always protect the rice.'

Back at the hotel, Tommy walks along the meandering path to his villa, wrapped in his own thoughts. And then, in a pool of light spilling across the path from lamps hidden deep in the grass, the woman is waiting for him. Her green and gold dress is lit from below, but the light's strength fails before it reaches her face. Behind her, the limbs of the banyan trees loom out of the darkness and Tommy's mind suddenly goes back to something his grandmother had told him.

'They call banyans 'strangler figs' in the west, you know. They grow on another tree, their seeds get into the cracks and crevices of the host tree and gradually they take it over.'

Suddenly, he understands: this is what is happening here, on this island. With all these new resorts and hotels and bars, Bali itself is gradually being taken over by an invasive species, a species of which he is a part.

The woman steps off the path and walks towards the rice field beyond. Tommy wants to shout after her but, before he can form the words, a breeze swells from the direction of the paddies, moving through the leaves of the banyan trees and the stalks of the rice plants. The noise of the wind dissolves into the sound of hammers striking metal, of gongs and cymbals, and Tommy's head is filled with images of the *wayang*, visions of spirits and goddesses, and battles between good and evil. In a trance, he follows the woman into the rice paddy, pushing through the waist high plants, deeper and deeper into the darkness.

In the morning Nina wakes from a fitful sleep. Her arm goes instinctively across towards Tommy but he isn't there and she sees that his side of the bed is undisturbed from the night before. The rest of the day passes in a blur as first the hotel staff and then police search in vain for her husband. And, while nobody says anything to her face, she is sure she hears them talking about the old man who disappeared after selling his rice field.

By early evening, Nina is frantic. As Rizal leads her back to reception to make another statement to the police, she passes the other guests who are watching a puppet show. This must be the shadow play that Tommy had talked about. A puppet of a young woman leads a male figure into what looks like a rice field. Nina is about to turn away when the male puppet's profile suddenly comes into sharp relief against the white sheet. The blood in her veins turns to ice: it's Tommy. He follows the figure of the woman into the rice field as the *gamelan* orchestra's chaotic harmonies, sounding more alien than anything she has ever heard, reach a climax. An army of warriors descends upon the male puppet and he is dragged down and disappears. At the edge of the stage, an old puppet master with a face carved from the hillside itself, turns and walks into the night.

Bladderwrack

Pauline Shearer

I wish I could say it was the perfume of roses or violets that haunted me. It was the smell of seaweed. Heaps of tangled, washed-up seaweed, entwined in my cellular memory, part of my DNA. They say smell is a pervasive sense, embedded into our recollections, the last to fade.

It has always been the same. From my first childhood visit to the sea, the aroma of seaweed has evoked a dark green primeval world, inhabited by shadowy forms.

The spring tide had exposed miles of beach that day. It had been a long early drive down to Cornwall. As soon as my bag was unpacked, I took my usual walk down to the sea. With the first deep breath of the salt-borne seaweedy air, my stride slowed with the rhythm of the waves.

I stopped to wiggle my toes in a rock pool. The sand gently sucked around the edges of my feet, drawing me downwards. Seagulls circled overhead emitting raw, ancient cries.

This time I was here with a purpose, to find my new home. The last meeting with my accountant had made it all too clear. The only viable aspect of my small bookshop, with flat above, was its property value. So I made myself redundant and told my elderly father I was moving to Cornwall.

'Ah, that would be the call of the seaweed,' he'd said, with a nod.

When I arrived at my afternoon appointment, the promised 'sea view' was a mere glimpse. Someone had once said there are 'cosy-in-the-valley' people and 'top-of-the-hill' people. Well, I was a 'beside-the-sea' person. I couldn't be this close and not see and breathe the ocean.

Next day, a damp, grey sea mist had swallowed the land. Just as I was about to leave my lodgings, the estate agent rang to cancel our appointment. This was not good. Completion on my property was just four weeks away. So I got in my car and started to drive. My new home was out there somewhere, I knew it. The view from the coast road on any other day would doubtless have restored my flagging spirits but not today. I like the mist, the feeling of being alone in the world. But today it just reflected my narrowing choices.

My eyes were starting to ache from peering into the mist when a weathered sign appeared, part buried in the hedge. *The Smugglers Arms – Good Home-Cooked Food.* An arrow pointed up a narrow road to my left. Well, I had time to waste and could do with something to lift my spirits, although the

invasive hedges on either side of the road did not look promising.

I must have been driving for about ten minutes, sides of the car fingered by brambles, when I saw a warm glow emanating from the windows of a large granite building materialising out of the mist. As I drove closer I could just make out the name: Smugglers Arms.

Inside, the smell of wood smoke greeted me as the landlord looked up from the beer glass he was drying. Soon sitting by the fire, I sipped the local crab soup and, being his only customer, the landlord leant on the bar and started to talk.

'So, you from upcountry then?'

I explained my grandparents had been Cornish, related to smugglers my dad had said, and I was looking for somewhere to live.

He looked thoughtful.

'Well now miss, Carter's place is on the market. Might suit you. Needs some work mind. Bit of history to that place. Still, if it's sea you're looking for, you couldn't do better than there.'

By the time I'd finished my soup he'd rung Jem Carter and it was agreed I could go and see the property just five minutes away.

The track from the pub to the cottage grew narrower and dropped steeply. As I drove slowly, the headlights reflected back off the mist and I could hear the grass brushing against the exhaust. I was growing increasingly nervous as to how I was going to get back up again.

Five minutes had turned into ten when the shape of a small cottage emerged. Before I could knock on the door, it opened and a man stepped out and took my hand in a rough grasp.

'It's a bit basic I'm afraid, miss. My grandmother's place this was. The water comes from the well but the electric was connected some years back.'

I noticed the bunches of rosemary, sage and lavender that hung from hooks on the ceiling. Memories returned of foraging alongside my mother for cold remedies, white frothy elderflowers, the pungent aroma of peppermint leaves and fine fern-like leaves of yarrow. Oh how I missed her but here she felt close.

'Knew her herbs did my gran. Would get right agitated if she ran out of her elderflower wine. Kept her safe, she said.'

There was a rag rug on the flagstone floor in front of a black range set in the large fireplace. It was a good-sized room that served as both kitchen and living room. At the windows, curtains printed with small, faded blue and yellow birds framed the mist. A wooden door led off to a small bathroom, a later addition. The open wooden staircase went up to a small landing with two bedrooms, one of which had been extended over the downstairs bathroom. I stood at the window of the bedroom and tried to discern forms in the distance but the mist was even denser. The cottage was isolated, yet already I could imagine myself living here. It was when we went outside that I noticed the large piles of seaweed beside the back door.

'Best thing for the garden,' Jem said with a knowing nod towards a small vegetable and herb garden surrounded by a protective hedge.

But I was only half listening, my attention taken by the sound of the sea. It seemed to be all round us.

'Is it far to the sea?'

'Can't you smell it?'

I sniffed. Yes of course. There it was. That smell of seaweed and salt. 'I'll take it,' I said. 'How soon can I move in?'

It took six weeks for the sale to go through but finally I was driving back down the track past the pub. It was as I took a steep turn that I saw the sea. I stopped the van. Despite the overcast sky, the sea still held that turquoise hue so typical of the Cornish coast. The vehicle had a higher clearance than my car but I had to carefully negotiate the deep potholes, which I'd somehow missed on my previous trip. The grass in the middle of the track had been cut down and the hedges trimmed back.

I pulled up outside the cottage and looked at my new home. It was a typical Cornish cottage. Large slabs of rough-hewn granite gave it a permanent and ageless feel. I took out the bunch of keys I'd collected from the solicitor and walked up to the old wooden door: remnants of pink, green, blue and yellow paint still clung to it. I liked it.

When I had negotiated the price I had agreed to buy some of the furniture. It belonged here. On the old pine table was a milk bottle with a bunch of daffodils and a note propped against a small parcel.

My grandmother left a package for whoever moved here. Just say if you need any help. Jem Carter.

I picked up the small, brown, wrinkled package held together with string. As I held the package in my hands, memories surfaced of parcels from my own grandparents, packaging telling stories of previous incarnations, everything recycled, nothing going to waste. It felt wrong to tear it open so I spent a while picking at the knots, until finally the string fell apart.

Inside was a faded notebook with fine spidery writing and small pencil drawings of what I assumed were herbs. I needed to escape from the packing boxes so I slipped the notebook into my fleece, pulled on my wellingtons and walked down the path that led to a small cove. The tide was out and I sat on a rock with the sun just beginning to break through the clouds, and started to thumb through the notebook but then I glanced

up and all I could think was, I am really here.

I bent down and touched the bronze strands of kelp, long slippery ribbons firm to the touch, coating my fingers with the smell of the sea. To the far side of the rock lay a heap of washed-up yellowy-green bladderwrack and egg wrack. I squeezed the bladders between my fingers hearing the familiar pop, a reminder of the bubblewrap waiting indoors. So I left the cove with its ruby rosettes of dulse and long thin strands of mermaids' hair and headed back to the cottage, the notebook tucked, once again, into the pocket of my fleece.

The rest of the day was spent unpacking and I was relieved to find that the range lit easily. By the evening, smells of supper filled the cottage. Before going up to bed, I lingered in the back doorway looking out over the calm sea, the full moon reflecting back with hardly a distortion. I was home.

When I went outside the following morning, it was the smell that alerted me. The piles of seaweed outside the back door had quadrupled in size. I'd not heard anyone walking on the gravel path. Where had it come from and more to the point, what was I going to do with it all?

Taking my mug of tea down to the cove, I found the notebook in the pocket of my fleece. The tide was coming in and I sat down at the edge of the path and started to look more closely at the delicate pages. Some of them were ingrained with small splash marks and hints of old smells. I recognised a few of the herbs as ones growing in the small garden. Turning over the pages I came to the unmistakable outline of bladderwrack, the seaweed now heaped high either side of the back door. At the bottom of the page there was a note.

Full moon. Use half on garden and return half to sea at noon and at dusk.

What could that be about? I shivered and noticed dark clouds gathering. With the wind now whisking sand across the cove, I headed back to the cottage.

The weather continued to deteriorate and the slates on the roof were soon rattling as the rain lashed at the windows. It wasn't until I went to turn on the light early that evening I realised there was no power. I knew I should have got some candles. Still there was a new battery in my torch, so I went to bed and snuggled down with my book.

I think it was the flash of lightening illuminating the curtainless room that woke me.

The crash of thunder seconds after had me wide awake. Rain beat against glass, the rapping of skeletal hands. It was the window latch flexing and groaning that caused my heart to lurch.

I felt a shiver run through me and clutched the duvet, willing its warmth to still my shaking body. It was then, at the second flash, that I saw the silhouettes of many dark forms pressed against the glass, gaping mouths filling the room with their wails. My heart pounded in my chest as I tugged the duvet over my head. My hands clasped my ears desperate to block out their cries, the endless lament: *seewee, seewee, seewee.*

Eventually, I fell asleep and it was nine o'clock before I stirred next morning. The wind had eased and a sea mist shrouded the landscape. I flicked a light switch but the power was still off. The fire in the range had gone out and I tried to tempt it back to life. Even with the day, the events of the storm stayed with me. I knew what I'd seen.

Determined not to have another evening without light, I decided to drive to the local post office to get some candles. The lull in the rain was over and the track was now a running stream. I turned the key in the car ignition but the engine refused to turn. For a moment I rested my head on the steering wheel, then got out and waded up the hill. Perhaps the landlord at the pub might have some spare candles.

The wind started to howl again but at least it cleared the mist a little. It was impossible to walk upright and I bent forward, steadying myself against the gusts. It was a relief to finally turn the corner at the top of the track, into the relative shelter of the hedges.

As I dried myself by the fire the landlord fetched me some candles and, despite my protests, insisted I drink a glass of elderflower wine.

'Forget the seaweed then?'

It was more of a statement than a question. So I asked him to explain.

'Goes way back. 1700 and 1800s I reckon. Smugglers in these parts, the Carters were. Some say they used seaweed to summon the wind and sea spirits if they saw a foreign ship on the horizon. They'd go down the shore, so the legends go, hold a long strand in their hand and whip it clockwise round they heads and whistle. Bad business it were, many souls driven on to the rocks by they lights in them storms.

'Hard times, mind. Folks round here needed all the help that came their way. Still, no good ever came from taking another man's life. A price had to be paid and it's said the elements claimed the lives of many an honest man about here thereafter.'

I shuddered, reminded of the night's events.

'Jessie, what lived in your cottage afore you, well, her husband was a fisherman. Good man, well-liked in these parts. Till one day, the spirits whipped up a storm, the like of which has never been seen here, before or since. Come out of nowhere folks say to claim another Carter soul.'

With each sip of the elderflower wine I felt myself relax and

71

the images of the previous night recede. I'd noticed the blossom by the cottage and made a mental note to look out a recipe. I settled back to listen.

'Jessie knew the old ways. After her husband were lost, it's said she summoned yon spirits and bargained with they to protect the lives of her boys and the other folk hereabouts.'

'I wish I'd met her,' I said.

'Reckon she'd have taken to you, miss.' The landlord nodded. 'But of late she would come up here on days like this, muttering about forgetting the seaweed. Real upset she'd be. Then she'd ask for a glass of my elderflower wine, said she'd used all hers, and then she'd be off, still muttering.'

'What had she forgotten to do with the seaweed?' I asked.

'Never did say miss, perhaps Jem'd know.'

Back in the cottage I dialed Jem Carter's number, as I'd not been able to find the fuse box. Apparently it was outside, obscured by the growing piles of seaweed. I asked if he knew where the seaweed came from but he said it had always been there after the full moon.

Despite the wind and the rain I slept well that night. As the sun shone through the window, I was woken by the sound of knocking at the back door. Hastily dressing, I ran downstairs to find Jem standing on the doorstep with a box of candles.

I invited him in for a cup of tea and he took off his boots and walked into the kitchen. He looked around, seemed pleased with what he saw and sat down at the table.

'You know, it's funny you saying about the seaweed. Got me thinking about they times when I was small and Gran took me down to the cove and we'd throw it into the sea. Something about it being a gift to the sea to keep the fishermen safe. I'd forgotten about it till you said.'

After Jem had gone, I went to the pocket of my old fleece

hanging on the hook by the door and brought out Jessie's notebook. I found the page with the bladderwrack, the note at the bottom written in that fine spidery writing. *Full moon. Use half on garden and return half to sea at noon and dusk.* Thumbing through, I came across a page with drawings of elderflowers and a recipe for elderflower wine and smiled to myself, as I settled down to read.

The sound of the kettle roused me and, walking past the open doorway, I was once again haunted by the smell of the fresh seaweed. I'd move some of that onto the garden after lunch. What was it my dad had said? It's the call of the seaweed. Mug in hand, I walked to the calendar and ringed the date of the next full moon.

The Bypass

Liz Crossland

Anna's eyes started to leak during dessert. Water swelled over her eyeliner, dripping off her nose into the crème brûlée. Mark passed a smeared napkin over the half-melted candle stuck in the Rioja bottle. Gravy and mascara mingled on her cheeks.

'Excuse me.'

She adjusted her skirt and shuffled to the Ladies. Mark reflected on their second date. Note to self, he thought. Don't mention the ex again. Spilt wine dripped from the table onto the floor.

The pub had a wood-burning stove. A whole log had smouldered before Anna returned. Mark was about to say goodnight when she sat down next to him in the window seat, tucked her leg over his and leant in to kiss him. She tasted of Malibu and Coke. He offered her a lift home.

Sinking into the heated seats of Mark's BMW, Anna ran her fingers over the leather padding. Her black lace tights stretched over her kneecaps so patches of skin were visible. Before turning the key in the ignition, Mark reached for her.

'Not here,' she said, indicating the white glare of the security lights in the car park.

Mark swung the car into reverse over the gravel. They joined the empty dual carriageway. To their left, houses sat: stone chunks. This was Stocksbridge, former mill town, buildings blackened by industry and coke fire. Mist spiralled through the streets, seeping and rising onto the grass verge. The car cruised along, dispersing fog with its headlights.

'Jesus!'

Mark veered but it was only a rabbit, stone-stricken in the bright light. Anna gripped his leg.

'Are you trying to get us killed?'

After twenty minutes, they pulled into Anna's estate. The house was modern and semi-detached. Mark left the engine running.

'Can I come in?' he said.

Anna chewed her lip.

'Can you give me a minute?'

She skipped out of the car, heading towards the front door, key fiddling for the lock. Mark inhaled before switching off the ignition.

He pushed through the doorway. Anna had disappeared. Standing on the doormat, he heard running water and realised she'd gone for a shower: she'd spilt wine as well as gravy down her top during the meal. Mark visualised her, naked under the cascading stream, soapy bubbles on her shoulders.

'I'll just make myself at home, then,' he called up the stairs.

And that's when he saw the shoes: Black patent, men's, size ten. Perched on a shoe-rack, shiny in the hall light. A formal double-breasted jacket hung from the coat hook, a college scarf cradled inside. Mark slung his own coat over the top and placed his shoes beside them on the rack.

The living room was cluttered: a pine bookcase, piano stacked high with books, coffee table spread with newspapers. No wonder Anna had never invited him in before. Mark's fingers itched to sweep the mess onto the floor. The only clear space was the black leather sofa. Sitting down, Mark's heels knocked against material. More clutter. He bent down and hooked his finger into another pair of men's shoes, concealed under the settee. Except these were slippers. Blue tartan slippers, worn at the heels and misshapen. Toes had filled these, knobbly toes, judging from the places where the fabric buckled up at the front. He turned the slippers over in his hands. Standard plastic soles, again size ten, ingrained with muck and coffee granules. Mark's feet were cold so he slipped them on. They were warm, as if the owner had just kicked them off.

The living room door flung open and Anna strode in, hair dripping. She'd changed into silk pyjamas. Mark put his hands

behind his head and stared. She had soap
bubbles stuck to her big toe.

'What the hell are you doing?' Anna said.

Water was dribbling from her hair and down
her top. Mark grinned.

'Imagining you in the shower.'

Anna indicated Mark's feet.

'These?' said Mark, "They were hidden under
the sofa."

Then, 'So you've got a secret boyfriend upstairs?'

Anna's eyes filled with tears. Great. Twice in one night. The slippers cushioned Mark's feet but at Anna's expression, he slid them back under the sofa. She stormed into the kitchen.

Mugs were clanking on a tray. Mark slunk through to help. He poured milk into a jug: it was cow-shaped, with a curved tail for a handle. Anna flicked the kettle on to boil. The bubbles formed through blue electric light. Mark wondered what he had done wrong. It was the slippers. That must be it. They'd taken her by surprise. But what about the neatly placed shoes, coat and scarf in the hallway? It wasn't until the kettle boiled that he saw the looped writing on the noticeboard.

'Remember the good times,' it said, message hazy with steam.

Anna turned to Mark.

'Sorry about before,' she said. 'It's just...you reminded me... wearing *his* slippers.'

Back in the lounge, Mark and Anna sat with thighs pressed together. Her pyjama legs were soft under Mark's fingers.

'God, you're gorgeous,' he said, hands roaming under her top. 'That other chap was mad to let you go.'

Anna frowned, turning to dip a digestive biscuit into her tea. It broke in half and floated just under the surface. Mark released his grip.

'So what's the deal with this guy? He just walked out without his shoes and coat? Left half his stuff?'

Anna bit her lip. 'Something like that.'

She waved her hand towards the piled books.

'All these books. Not mine. The newspapers: not mine. Even the cow jug...'

Mark looked at the porcelain tail and face. He liked the vomiting cow: the way it spewed milk out of its mouth when poured.

They stared at the living room, at the stacks of paperbacks.

There were Penguin copies of *Lolita*, *Brave New World*, *Brideshead Revisted*. Most of the hardbacks were new: *Palin's Europe*, *Jamie's 30-Minute Meals*.

'You could sell them,' Mark said, 'or keep the ones you like. Or tell him to hire a van and get his stuff the hell out of your house.'

Anna fished the tea-soaked biscuit out of her mug.

'I wish it was that simple,' she said, knuckles whitening as she gripped the handle.

'Or hire a skip,' said Mark, wondering what was so difficult about getting rid of someone else's crap.

The tartan slippers were beckoning to Mark from under the settee. When Anna popped through to the kitchen for another biscuit, he slipped them on, shuffling his toes around until they fit. From the coffee table, Mark picked up a sheath of paper covered in jerky hand-written notes. He began to read.

Anna stood open-mouthed in front of Mark, digestive biscuits crumbling in her hands.

Mark showed her the paper.

'At the very least, you could throw this in the bin.'

He crumpled it in his hand.

'You should get rid of this. It can't be healthy.'

Anna glared at his feet. She whipped the slippers away and flung them into a corner.

'Ever heard of bin bags?' Mark said.

As she marched upstairs, Mark glanced down at his own mug. The remains of a digestive biscuit were drowning in milky tea, a clog of sogginess. He'd pushed it too far, but really…what was Anna doing with this hoard of possessions? He longed for his BMW and the comfort of his minimalistic studio flat but his eyes were heavy, toes cold on the laminate floor. He reached out to pull the slippers back towards him and shuffled into them. Warmth enveloped his feet. They were a better fit than before,

the protruding lumps less noticeable. Yes, he'd keep the slippers. But the rest of the junk needed to go.

Anna was creaking around on the floor above his head. He'd go up in a minute when she'd calmed down. Mark shut his eyes. Dozing, the scrapes became branches of trees groaning in the wind. Yes, he was driving. Travelling alone on the Stocksbridge Bypass. The fog had thickened into ghost's breath, the mist forming shapes in the dips on the road. Here: a flurry of houses. There: a mug of swirling coffee, an arm, a hand, a whole man, naked except for slippers and a black coat. No face. Stacks of books surrounded him. Mark slammed his foot down on the accelerator but the man had gone.

Mark jolted awake, arm bent, foot in a driving position. He peeled the slippers from his feet and skidded them under the sofa. He picked his way past the piled-up books and went upstairs.

Anna was half-asleep, her breathing ragged.

'Don't turn the light on.'

Mark lowered himself onto the bed.

'Don't make me drive back home over that moor,' he said.

He reached over and stroked her hair. Her face was wet. He kissed her cheekbones, licking off the salt until she relaxed in his arms and her heart rate steadied. Mark tried to slow his own breathing but he was gulping air. The memory-foam mattress was uncomfortable. His elbow protruded into bulges in the bed which seemed unwilling to mould to his shape. After an hour of shifting his weight, he found the right dents to encase his body and fell into a slumber.

He dreamt he was falling. Dropping through trees and towards a moving car. He plunged through the roof of his own BMW and into the back seat. The driver's hands were skeletal sticks protruding from the sleeves of a black coat. The feet controlling the pedals were slipper-shod with knobbly ankles.

Please don't look in the rear-view mirror, he thought. Don't meet my eyes. Bile raised in his throat. Crumbs of digestive biscuits covered the seat; pools of milky tea formed in leather crevices. He gasped, noticing the figure on the road in front of them.

'Watch out!' Mark screamed.

The driver's head turned. Except it wasn't a human head. It was the mouth of the porcelain cow jug. It tipped and vomited cold milk over him.

The alarm rang. As sunshine crept under unfamiliar curtains, Mark realised his chest was soaked with sweat. He was almost stuck to the bed. He could stay here, sink into the insulating foam of the mattress which embraced him. Then, he felt Anna trembling.

'Babe.'

He hauled himself from the grip of the bed and cradled her as she sat up, arms wrapped around knees.

'I didn't want you to know. I can't get rid of it. His stuff. Everywhere.'

Mark saw what he had missed in the darkness of the previous night. Cardboard boxes piled high, almost to the ceiling. He dug his fingers into the memory-foam mattress. Anna's shoulders were shaking.

'Let me help you,' he said.

He flung open the wardrobe. A mesh of wires and plastic. Three computers, amplifiers, speakers: a tangle of electrical equipment loaded from floor to the wardrobe rail. Anna's clothes hovered over the jumble apologetically. Her eyes were blank.

'Look under the bed.'

Boxes of vintage cameras, lenses, lens caps and unused film. A mouldy packet of digestive biscuits.

'How many cameras does he have?'

'45,' she said. 'You've not seen the study.'

On the way to work, the bypass was busy. Mark gripped the gear stick and blinked, the unwanted junk from Anna's house in his mind, interfering with his vision. Camera cases merged with electric wiring and half-eaten digestive biscuits floated across his retina. Crumbs. There were crumbs in the folds of his boxer shorts. They dug into his skin against the seat.

Later, after a boring meeting, Mark turned the car in the direction of Stocksbridge. He'd promised to go back. Mist was creeping up from the heather at the side of the road, snaking across Mark's headlights. 88mph, 95mph. The fog was shifting. He could see piles of books and outstretched arms. Mark drove straight through those swirling forms and arrived shaking at Anna's.

The black patent shoes were still there, and the coat and scarf. Two coats, in fact.

'Not made it to the charity shop yet,' Mark said.

Anna grimaced. In the living room, the coffee table was more cluttered than before. Books had been added to the piles. The tartan slippers were peeping out from under the settee. When Anna went through to the kitchen, he pulled them on. His hands found a book; he flicked through the pages until the spine bent open onto a familiar page covered in handwriting.

Anna was standing in front of Mark, mugs of steaming tea in her hand.

'Not again,' she said.

Mark frowned.

'The rest of it's just junk, but these slippers are comfy.'

The slippers clung to his feet but he pulled them off, shoving them under the sofa along with the book. Anna plonked the tea down, offered Mark a digestive biscuit and tucked her feet under her legs. Mark draped his arm across her shoulders.

'So what's the deal with your ex, then? Some sort of psycho?

Or kleptomaniac? Or psycho-kleptomaniac?'

Anna giggled.

'A bit of both. I found 40 undeveloped films in the freezer. Hidden under frozen peas.'

They made a plan of action. Step one: clear all cupboards, wardrobes and drawers. Step two: box everything. Step three: contain everything in the study. It was over the coats, scarf and shoes that they had the argument. Anna wanted them left in the hall.

'He might need them,' she said, eyes welling.

The drizzle became a torrent. Sending her off for a shower, Mark scooped the soggy clump of tissues into a pile and deposited them in the kitchen bin. His eyes fell on the notice-board and the inked message about the *good times* in that same looped writing. He rubbed his sleeve across the text but the marks wouldn't budge. Mark went into the hall. The shoes were there, sparkling black. And four coats, two scarves.

He climbed the stairs. Anna was in bed, brushing her hair. Boxes loomed, casting shadows onto the mattress, the grooves made by his body the night before still visible. Mark sank into them. Crumbs were collected in the ridges, rough under his fingers.

'You been eating digestive biscuits in here?' he said.

Anna snorted and moulded her body around him. Flicking the crumbs away, Mark let himself be pulled down into the mattress, taking his place.

Mark woke up, dripping in sweat. A nightmare: something about vomiting cows in black coats and college scarves, stored in boxes of biscuits. He remembered driving. He remembered eyes: his own eyes looking at him from the back seat. And a man. Standing in front of him in the road. A man in a coat. Faceless. And slippers. Slippers on his feet. Slippers that slid off the pedals when he tried to brake.

Anna turned and noticed the sweat on his brow.

'You're boiling up,' she said, wiping his forehead.

He had a fever, she told him. He needed to stay in bed: he should ring in sick.

Anna left for work, slamming the door. Mark's eyes started to flicker. Memories of fog from the Stocksbridge Bypass floated in his brain. Tendrils of mist dissolved so he could see ankles. A pair of tartan slippers blurred his vision. The boxes arching over the bed threatened to topple. He'd sleep on the sofa instead. On the back of the door was a man's dressing gown. He wrapped it round his shoulders: it smelt of coffee and perspiration.

On the coat hook at the bottom of the stairs, four coats had become six. Another college scarf had joined the other two, snaking around the pegs. Mark blinked, trying to refocus his eyes and his mind.

In the living room, he put his slippers on: they nestled his feet. Settling on the sofa with the hidden paperback, he tried to lull himself back towards sleep. But the book kept falling open at the same page. The jerky looped writing. Black and italic. He flung the book on the floor; it skidded then stopped.

Then he saw it. The black coat flickering past the window. He blinked his eyes. The book was at his feet again. He picked it

up. It was that same page. Then, the tap at the window. A black sleeve. The slippers squeezed his feet. The door banged. The letter-box clattered. A black coat was disappearing up the drive.

Mark went into the hall. The shoes glistened, newly polished. Seven black coats were piled, coat on coat, scarves threaded through the arm holes, winding round the neck of each. His slippers tightened on his feet like a vice: he couldn't prise them off. They were truly his now. Mark stumbled back into the living room.

Anna found him later, passed out on the sofa, covered in biscuit crumbs. He was dreaming of the Stocksbridge Bypass, of course he was, with its God-forsaken ghosts and old wives' tales. She shook the sleeve of his dressing gown.

'Wake up,' she said.

His eyes snapped open. She paled and backed away.

'You look just like him,' she said.

Mark straightened, annoyed.

'Your ex was here today. Knocking on the door, scaring me silly. I'm ill, you know. Tomorrow I call the police. Then we tell him about his stuff. Either he hires a van and collects it, or we sell it, give it to charity, whatever.'

Anna was chalk-white.

'That's impossible,' she said.

'Why?' he said.

'Because he's dead. Killed on the Stocksbridge Bypass.'

Mark didn't remember leaving the house. But he did recollect trying to pull off the slippers. They were welded to his feet. In the hallway, he pulled one of the eight coats from the hook. It slithered round his shoulders.

He was in the car, the air-conditioning sending ice cold blasts onto his neck. His hairy ankles were bare as he changed gear, pressing the soles of his slippers hard on the clutch. Mist hit the windscreen. He passed the town of Stocksbridge. Fog pulled at the wing mirrors, depositing watery smoke on his windscreen. The wipers had failed but he put his foot down. He'd shatter those shifting shapes if he had to.

Then he sees the eyes. The carved-out crevices of his own eyes from his dream in the rear-view mirror. They widen as if to say, Watch out!' but it is too late. He's already swerved to avoid the man in the black coat.

The Ghosts of Havisham Manor

Rebecca Lloyd

D ennis could hear the film crew setting up behind him. He was standing in an ornate window bay in the hall of a large manor house, waiting for his call. The dreary noise of the crew, echoing against the wood panelling, was cut through by constant prickly questions from the presenter, Martha. Dennis wondered how she would cause difficulties for everyone this time. He always referred to Martha as The Old Botox Trout in conversation with his close friends, and he complained about her to his spirit guide, the Swami.

Dennis frequently reminded the Swami of the burdens he suffered as resident medium on The Haunted Homes of Britain, where the production values were constantly undermined by Martha's preening obsession with her ratings and stardom. Dennis was convinced that when they were filming in the dark cellars of Fellfield Hall the previous month, he had seen her use a stick to prod the sound recordist in the back. The poor man had screamed and nearly dropped his microphone boom.

Dennis could see why viewers had found the film compelling evidence of ghosts because, after editing, it appeared to be a genuine encounter with the spirit world. There was certainly no doubt that, as his gaping face loomed in close-up, green hued in the infra-red light, the sound man had been truly scared. For Dennis, the disappointment was that he had been frightened by a living soul, and not one of the departed.

'Do you work here? Are you the local guide for this place? Are you supposed to show us round? What's your name?'

Turning, Dennis saw Martha gesturing at a small thin man who was standing beside a carved stone fireplace, staring at them.

'Madam, I am Christopher Sydney,' the man said quietly and looked around at the crew, pausing only to observe the baggage spilt over the floor.

Then he turned and slowly walked towards the far end of the

hall and Dennis saw that they had been dismissed, unworthy of further consideration.

Dennis peered at Sydney as he wandered away, vague and then solid, moving in and out of the streaming sunlight from the windows so that Dennis found it hard to be certain of him. There was a neat dark goatee that Dennis had seen and some sort of oversized white collar but the clothing somehow seemed more a set of impressions than definite articles. Some people simply have no idea how to style themselves, he thought, or perhaps those who work in places like this prefer to blend in, dressing up to show they are part of the house. Dennis decided that the beard was just a dreary little affectation and he pursed his mouth.

He concluded that Sydney was one of those who used their employment in old houses as a badge of belonging. In rare agreement, Dennis and Martha were irritated by the clerks and guides who resented visitors, guarding history as if their lives depended on it. They had caused problems before, the dusty obsessives whose fragments of knowledge were their weapons against the world. Some house guides became quite excited about being filmed but others were reluctant, always complaining about the crew and droning on about historical accuracy.

Dennis had a strong sense that Sydney was one of those who refused to see any importance in filming haunted houses. Although he had some sympathy with them, considering Martha's exploits, Dennis felt that the guides did not realise ghosts were like gold dust, and just as valuable, and that the public visited these old houses on their coach tours because they were happy to pay to be frightened out of their skins. Some people were only interested in history if they thought that there was some horror in it. That was the reason, after all, for the popularity of Haunted Homes. It was never about truth and accuracy, but history on the cheap, the past as a thrill, packaged for the viewer safe at home.

The production company had recently brought a parapsychologist onto the team, a university lecturer specialising in the paranormal. Each programme now had a closing segment of Dr Curtis reviewing the filmed events in a serious, dispassionate way that implied credible investigation as well as entertainment. Dennis quite liked Curtis, who had a rigorous interest in what they were doing and, although he was the sceptic to Dennis the believer, he clearly thought that it was all worthwhile.

Curtis had spent a considerable amount of time asking Dennis for the details about how he contacted the Swami, although for some time Dennis felt compelled to evade such direct questions. He finally admitted that he encountered the presence of his spirit guide only occasionally when he went into a trance, as the Swami was unpredictable.

Curtis had seemed neither worried nor surprised by this, concluding his questions with a silent nod. Dennis knew that Curtis had studied recordings of the trances. It was always a popular part of the programme, when Dennis reclined on a chair, chin up, lips trembling, and his right hand waving, reaching and patting the air as the Swami directed him so that he could inform the viewers which spirits were likely to be present. Curtis told Dennis that he had never seen anything like it, and Dennis felt rather flattered.

Although Sydney was now coming back across the hall towards them, Dennis ignored him and turned back to Martha who was going through the filming schedule with everyone.

'As we've already got the exterior shots, I want to get the general interior stuff over with now,' she said. 'We'll film the Havisham Manor person first, so that we can be rid of him by the end of the day. Do you have anything interesting for us?' She looked at Sydney, who stood in the shadows close to the crew.

He ignored the question, and just looked directly at Martha.

'We need some info about the house and the ghosts,' she said.

'The viewers will want to hear about who's died here, you know, to get the historical perspective, and preferably if they did it in some horrible way, so that we can say why they're haunting the place. Is there a screaming nun or, even better, a blubbering kid?'

When he continued to stand in silence, Martha said, 'Really, didn't you get any information from the office?' She peered at him and sighed.

Dennis, knowing how Martha responded to any perceived snub, wondered if she might break into one of her tantrums and have Sydney removed from the house. But she seemed uncertain about how to deal with him.

'Darling?' She turned instead to the director who was carrying a big case into the hall. 'Didn't someone let them know what we were going to need?'

'I thought it was all taken care of,' he said. 'But I've got some rough notes here, if they help.' And he passed them to an assistant, who handed them to Martha.

'Anyway, I've been working on those plans with Curtis, if you remember?'

He nodded at Martha, a gesture that Dennis found hard to understand.

Then the team broke apart, organising their individual tasks. Dennis, thinking that he should help himself and the Swami get into the right mood before filming started, told them that he was going to get a feel for the place and Martha stared at him for a few moments. Then he realised that Sydney was standing close behind her and that he too was watching him. Dennis started quickly up the wide, wooden staircase. Suddenly, but not knowing why, he wanted to leave the hall very much.

The medium wandered along the deeply carpeted corridor, trying unyielding door handles until one gave. The small bedroom he found was sun filled and airy, a peaceful place after the discomfort he had felt in the hall. He went to the window.

Below, the gardens of low trimmed box hedges spoke to him of the order of the past, of ruffed collars, long silk skirts and Elizabethan heroes with swirling capes, making romantic, deep sweeping bows to their ladies. How beautiful history could be in a place like this. Even the tragedies had a charm that turned their ghosts into lovely stories, he thought, turning back to the room.

Then he saw a leather notecase on a small side table and picked it up, realising with some pleasure that it contained a history of the house. It was just the thing to read so that the Swami could absorb a sense of Havisham Manor, so that when he spoke through Dennis later, on camera, the medium would impress with a necessary authority about the place and inhabitants. It was not fakery but proper research. No harm in making sure about a place. He took out his pouch of herbal pills, swallowed one and began to read.

The team had gathered together again in the hall to record Dennis's trance session. He sat in a carved wooden chair taken from beside the stone fireplace, although it was so uncomfortable that getting into the trance took some time. Closing his eyes, he concentrated so that all he could hear was the low whirr of the camera. The herbal pills were having their full effect now and Dennis was very relaxed. He closed his eyes, and his hand fluttered up and then the voice of the Swami came through.

Although it was not always possible to be certain about the precise location of his accent, the Swami always sounded authentically Indian to the viewers and today he was in full flow. He recounted the scraps of the lives of the past, of Roman soldiers who walked the grounds, of the ghost of the debauched Second Earl. He had been a heartless, cruel drunkard who had even thrown his own daughter to his hunting dogs for daring to challenge his authority.

Then, through Dennis, the spirit guide spoke in great detail

of Maria Ail. Poor tragic Maria had been a servant girl who had loved a young man from the village but he had abandoned her, along with their baby. Unable to face their lives of suffering, the Swami continued, she had thrown herself and the child from the roof of the great house and they were doomed to walk the corridors crying forever. Then Dennis started to cough, his voice harsh and rough. Finally his guide seemed to withdraw in exhaustion, allowing Dennis to return from the trance.

As the crew packed up their kit and took their leave, Dennis was struck by the faces of Martha and the director. He had never seen them smile after one of his sessions.

'Was that alright?' he asked, surprising himself with a need for reassurance.

'Oh, it was very alright,' said Martha, laughing. 'You did just what we wanted.' She paused and then said, 'You are finished. We've got you talking a load of rubbish on camera, and we can prove that you are nothing but a cheat.'

'What do you mean?' said Dennis.

The director stepped forward and leant over him. 'Curtis put some fake history bits mixed up with some genuine stuff in a file that he left where you could find it. All we had to do was film you regurgitating the crap and have Curtis record a segment exposing you and get the lot to the papers.

'You're just so stupid you didn't know the difference between the real and the made-up bits. Curtis thinks that you're just a snivelling little mincing idiot who gets high on Indian dope pills and believes he can speak to the dead.'

He paused and then, 'Didn't you wonder why the rooms upstairs were all locked when you went off to commune with your bloody guru? You made it so easy. Oh, and Maria Ail is an anagram, by the way. God knows why the public like you so much but you're not what we want on the show. It's supposed to be about Martha, not you.'

He stopped again, then laughed and said, 'Is your hair real?'

'Well, I've always thought that he's been wearing a rug,' said Martha, artfully brushing her sleeve then looking at Dennis. 'He's so vain. But darling, can we please make sure that the next medium is a proper one and not some little old drama queen?'

The director nodded, and they swept away together up the stairs.

'I've seen you faking it,' Dennis shouted up to them. 'This whole show is a fix. You wouldn't know a ghost if it slapped you in the face.'

They laughed and crossed the landing, and Dennis rushed up the stairs after them. His throat was hot, starting to constrict him. This was not over, he thought, and he would not let them get away with it. He did not want to leave the show.

'Martha, wait,' he called to her. 'Martha, please.'

As he trotted along the open corridor after her, he was stopped by an urge to look down into the hall. When he did, he saw that the only person there was Christopher Sydney.

Sydney was staring up at him.

Dennis was aware of silence thickening around him. The constriction in his throat tightened and his eyes pricked. Then he could hear Martha's voice and he turned his head to find where she was. He suddenly craved her practical presence, wanting her to ward off whatever was making this strange stillness that closed in on him. She was so much stronger than he was.

He looked down towards Sydney but Sydney was no longer in the hall. He was now at the top of the stairs, directly facing him and there seemed to be something beside him, shifting slightly as he watched it, forming and reforming. Then it became an identifiable shape, appearing as a shaven-headed man in a loose white robe, which threw into relief his dark skin.

Dennis felt that he should recognise the figure, that he was supposed to know him but he was certain that he had never seen this man before. The two were moving towards him now and his stomach clenched.

They were drifting onwards without touching the ground and he realised that although he knew that they were looking at him, he could not clearly see their eyes. The points of their faces, eyes, nose and mouth, were all smudges. Nothing certain.

Nausea rose in him. He turned, lurching down the corridor where Martha and the director had gone.

He found them standing close together in a small room. Martha's initial disdain on seeing Dennis burst in shifted into curiosity when she saw his wildness.

'For God's sake,' she started to say but, as he rushed to the wall furthest from the door, she looked askance.

'What is it? What's going on?' she said. Then, 'What the hell's happening? Why's it so bloody cold?'

Dennis looked up and realised that Sydney and the Indian were in the room with them. He yelled out, 'It's him. It's Christopher Sydney. He's doing this.'

As he said it, he saw Sydney move towards Martha, still not walking but somehow sliding over the floor, coming to a stop in front of her. It seemed to be getting darker there, as if no light could ever be where they were, as if Martha and Sydney were in a place where nothing should exist.

Martha was moaning. Dennis could just see that her mouth was hanging open, slack-jawed just as the sound man had been. She was losing command of her body to her fear and that was what scared Dennis the most. There could be no protection. Her self-assurance and arrogance were useless.

The director was a snivelling bundle in the corner of the room and, for a moment, Dennis remembered what he had said about them not knowing ghosts. He realised that he too did not know ghosts. He had thought that they were victims, badly treated in life and then doomed and restless in death but he had never really seen them as perpetrators of horror.

Sydney was a ghost of Havisham Manor, that dreadful old Earl who always wanted his own way in everything and he had never been a good man. Nothing that emanated so much darkness could have ever been good.

Whatever was with Martha now was consuming her, wiping her out. In the air around them, Dennis thought that he could hear crying, shouting, laughing, starting to fade. Empty, broken sounds drifting out of the living world.

And then the Indian was beside Dennis. He turned and looked at the figure, at the sockets and gaps in the face that showed through transparent and filmy skin.

Dennis heaved and his guts twisted as he realised that this was the Swami. I just made him up, he thought. I'm sure I did. But he's here. Is he smiling? Oh God, he's smiling. Oh God, he's touching me.

Dennis called out, 'No, no. I'm sorry, Swami. I didn't mean to be bad, and I didn't mean to make all those things up. Oh no, please, no.'

There was silence as the voices in the air faded away altogether into the darkness and the Swami smiled and took his hand.

Forget-Me-Not

Donna Painter

Do you believe in ghosts? I do. I've seen one.

When I was ten years old, Gran was admitted to hospital for an operation; the details of which I cannot remember. I do recall Mam's displeasure at Gran having to recuperate at our house. Her exact words were, 'We'll never get rid of her now.'

And, by God, she was right. For after Gran's death, and for weeks after she had been lowered into the grave to rest alongside Grandpa Kane, we still couldn't get rid of her.

I remember Mam and Dad arguing.

'Why can't your Billy have her? She's his bloody mother as well.'

'Because I'm the eldest. Besides, Billy lives in Swansea. We live two streets away. My mother was born in Wattstown, and if she's going to die, she's going to die in Wattstown.'

And that was that.

We lived in an ordinary terraced house and my bedroom was at the top of the stairs; the walls a neglected drab colour. I shared it with the airing cupboard and gurgling hot water pipes which, prior to Gran moving in, didn't disturb me.

My scanty furnishings consisted of a wardrobe, a dressing table, a single bed, and a pair of faded curtains that hung lank and lifeless and failed to reach the skirting-board. Yet, despite its dreariness, I was possessive of it. It was the place in which I whiled away my happiest hours. Living the dreams and nightmares of others. Wishing I too were orphaned and could go to Lowood Institute along with Jane Eyre.

'Why must I share with Maggie misery guts?'

'Don't call your sister that.'

'Well, why can't Gran go home after her operation?'

'Look. Your father's spoken. She's having your bedroom and I don't want to hear another word.'

'I hope she dies in hospital.'

And, as I slammed the living room door, the little glass panes trembled in their frames.

After being discharged from Porth Cottage Hospital, Gran and her commode infiltrated my bedroom. The stench of camphor and ammonia lingered in every recess of the house. I resented being forbidden to read at night for fear of disturbing my miserable sister with whom I now had to share a room. The only pleasure to arise from the situation was that Mam and I appeared united in our loathing of Gran and I was cheered at becoming Mam's confidante.

Apparently, when my parents started courting, Dad was betrothed to a woman called Shirley. He broke off their engagement and announced his intention to marry Mam. It seemed Gran favoured Shirley and never warmed to Mam – or to me for that matter. For several years after Mam and Dad were married, Mam wasn't permitted to visit Gran on a Wednesday. Wednesday was Shirley's day to visit. Gran also disapproved of my being called Mary after my maternal grandmother and Maggie, who at Dad's behest bears Gran's name of Margaret Elizabeth, became Gran's pet.

Mam also made me privy to her notion that anyone over the age of seventy should be taken up the mountain and shot. I sensed Mam's rapture at the prospect of dragging Gran's debilitated body up to Llanwonno and putting a bullet deep into that marble-veined skull. And, had it meant the repossession of my bedroom, I would have pulled the trigger myself.

Do you know what haunted me most about Gran whilst she was still alive (for there were many things that came to haunt me later)? It was her flesh, which on occasion I was forced to touch. Dad would sit her in the armchair next to the hearth and she would croak away with the fire's spit and crackle. I was transfixed by the shock of shapeless hair swept across her sallow scalp, held fast by a white hairpin. Her skeleton wore its flesh like an ill-fitting shroud and with her being hard of hearing, I'd

pat her arm to get her attention, making us both jump.

I wasn't afraid of Gran. But her eye lids didn't flutter open like someone just waking from sleep. They snapped open, revealing two cavernous depressions and a glacial stare that looked through and beyond me. Her sagging skin would shift sideways. It was like losing my fingers in layers of crumpled tissue to find them poking into a vein of warm blood.

Sharing a bed with a five year old was uncomfortable and most nights I thrashed about in the delirium of a vivid, recurring dream, in which all my teeth were being extracted.

'Dreaming of teeth is a sign of death,' Mam said. 'Gran must be on her way out.'

And, as if to confirm Mam's premonition, next door's black Labrador took to howling through the night.

Maggie was too young to understand the foreboding, but I was drawn to death. I'd stand inside the bedroom when Mam was in attendance, gripped by Gran's suffering, listening to her cries of 'Dear God,' and 'Oh Mam,' spellbound by her blue parched lips and the rattle in her throat.

After several nights of black-dog-howling, I awoke one morning to discover Gran's bedroom door shut. Dad was sitting at the kitchen table. There were no tears. I felt nothing but curiosity and a twinge of relief that I could have my bedroom back and read my books in peace. I had no inkling at the time that peace was to desert our household.

'Can I see the body?'

And it strikes me now how, in the space of one night, Gran had suddenly become a body.

'You'll have to ask your father.'

Dad rose, taking my hand in his as if I were an ally. He escorted me through the dank and dingy passage, where strips of mouldy, green-and-black-leafed wallpaper did their utmost to cling to the walls. He opened the bedroom door and I hovered in the centre of the room, grabbed by the power of death. Gran lay draped in a white sheet. A brace propped up her chin, keeping her jaw shut. Her face was peaceful and placid. I had no expectation of her eyelids snapping open and her glassy eyes staring through me. I returned to the kitchen jubilant.

'That's the best I've ever seen her.'

'Did you touch her?' Mam asked.

'No. I only looked.'

'You're supposed to touch the corpse,' Mam said, 'or it will come back to haunt you.'

After the funeral, Dad presented Mam with Gran's wedding ring – a gold band of forget-me-nots; each delicate flower fused to the next.

'If you think I'm wearing that you've got another thing coming. I'll keep it for our Maggie. She's the only bugger your mother liked.'

It was several days later I reclaimed my bedroom. I refused to sleep in my bed, Gran's death bed, with a resolve I never knew I possessed. I was rewarded with Gran's old bed, retrieved from her house when Dad sorted through her effects.

Ensconced in my bedroom that first evening, I was unnerved. The smell of camphor still permeated the walls. It leached between the layers of crocheted wool. With each rustle of the page, my eyes peered over the top of my book, first at the door and then in the direction of the rumbling pipes, expecting to see I know not what. I shuddered, trying to ignore how Miss Havisham reminded me of Gran, laid out on the bed, my bed – an image, now forty years on, still etched in my memory – and I welcomed the summons downstairs to a supper of milk and Welsh cakes. The aroma of griddled currants refreshed my nostrils.

I finished supper, bid Mam a goodnight and made my way upstairs with a stab of trepidation. Standing in the open doorway, my fingers fumbled along the interior wall in search of the light switch. I depressed it. There was a fissure of light. A flash. And I was plunged into darkness.

'What the devil...?' Mam was at the foot of the stairs. 'You'll wake Maggie.'

'The bulb. It's gone.'

'Be quiet. I'll fetch a new one from the outhouse.'

I descended the stairs with haste; an uneasy feeling rising from the depths of my insides at the thought of remaining on the threshold of my bedroom.

Mam climbed upon the bed – the headboard of which was against the left wall as you looked in from the doorway – and inserted the bulb.

'Right. Try it.'

I pressed the switch. The light came on and Mam stepped down.

'Now go to sleep.'

She paused while I buried myself before extinguishing the light and closing the door.

I cannot say what disturbed my sleep, except that I shivered to waking with a clammy brow and a feeling of unease. My bladder was about to burst. I lit the bedside lamp and crept out of bed. It is with slight embarrassment that I tell you I had a pink plastic chamber pot underneath my bed, the inside of which had become crusted white with bleach.

I knelt on the floor. My hand searched for the handle and I extracted the chamber. As my eyes drew level with the mattress, they fell upon two shafts of withered flesh, ugly bone-bruised feet and curled-up yellow claws. I recoiled, my back hitting the flat, hard surface of the wardrobe. Gran lay there in her shroud, her chest bones protruding, her throat sucked-in, her shock of straw-white hair escaping, and her raw-red sockets gaping at the ceiling.

I stood mute on the spot for what felt like an age but could only have been a second.

I was unaware that I had crossed the shadowy landing, or that a warm trickle had run down my legs, until I returned to the bedroom with Mam to find the bed empty and a wet patch on the carpet in front of the wardrobe.

'There. It was a bad dream.'

'Can I sleep with Maggie?'

'No. Don't be such a baby. Go back to bed.'

The following night, half-asleep, half-awake, I thought I heard the breath of the wind in my room. The air chilled. Needles pricked my skin as cold, blue flesh brushed my hand. Paralysed, I watched the blankets lifting and felt the gnarled yellow toe nails scraping my bare legs as Gran climbed into my bed. Straw-white strands jabbed at my face. I heard the screech of a terror-stricken soul, not realising the cry had escaped from my own throat.

Mam burst through the door and I sobbed in her arms whilst she convinced me it had been a nightmare. She continued to stroke my head as I lay back down. Then, I felt her hand still and her body stiffen as she withdrew a white metal hairpin from my pillow.

I was kept home from school the following morning and, when Dad left for work, Mam and I went to St Paul's to seek the help of Father Glyn. I was instructed to wait in the vestry while they were in congress. When they emerged, Father Glyn accompanied us on our short walk home to Bailey Street.

Father Glyn followed Mam and I upstairs and sat down on my bed. Mam passed him Granny Mary's bible. He balanced it on the palm of his hand, took his crucifix from around his neck and placed it on top of the black leather cover. He bowed his head and proceeded to speak with God, asking Him to lift the forces of evil and cleanse my soul of the devil.

I hadn't realised until that moment that my young soul had been violated, so I bent my head and hung on to the words of The Lord Is My Shepherd, a psalm I was familiar with from school. When Father Glyn began to chant The Lord's Prayer, Mam mumbled it with him, and I, head still bent in solemnity, joined in with Amen.

The exorcism failed and each night I was disturbed by Gran, my family's sleep was disturbed by me.

One tea time, after a lifetime of sleepless nights, Maggie came down from upstairs.

'Don't worry, Mary. Gran won't bother you no more.'

'What are you talking about, Maggie?' asked Mam.

'I saw Gran. She was lying on Mary's bed. So I took her into my bedroom.'

Mam and Dad dashed upstairs. I followed and Maggie trailed behind. There was an indentation on my bed: a hollow on the pillow where Gran's head had been and, along the bed, a slight oppression where Gran's ghostly figure had set down. And if anyone else inhaled the smell of death, they kept it to themselves.

I slept easier thereafter. Whether it was due to Maggie or the result of continuous sleep deprivation, I couldn't say. However, this ominous matter was not yet laid to rest: Mam's concerns were now for Maggie.

Maggie had taken to playing upstairs and, alone in her room, could be heard in conversation. When confronted, she announced she was talking to Gran. It was only then I noticed that Maggie had the same fly-away hair as Gran. And that she had taken to pulling it across her head and fixing it with her doll's hair-slide.

Maggie's reluctance to leave her room secretly pleased me but Mam, fearing for Maggie's well-being, was determined to rid us of malevolence. She whispered to me details of her appointment with a medium – not that I knew what a medium was – a woman called Mrs Chislett of Chepstow Road, Treorchy. She was to go on the bus as Treorchy was about fifteen miles from our home, in another valley.

When she returned, she went up to her bedroom and came down wearing Gran's forget-me-not ring.

Mam told me how she had paid Mrs Chislett two pounds at the front door and was led through the house into a dimly-lit parlour. She had sat opposite Mrs Chislett, at a round table covered with a red cloth, and waited in silence while the medium went into a trance. Mam was asked for a treasured possession and offered up the crooked thruppence which she kept in the zipped compartment of her purse.

The medium had described Gran in appearance and told Mam that Gran was in the room with them. You have a ring belonging to the deceased, Mrs Chislett had said. She wants you to wear it. She is telling me you have proved yourself dutiful, for which she has never shown you a kindness. She is sorry for it, and is asking you to wear her ring.

In adulthood I moved away from the valley and neglected to keep in touch with my family. I saw Mam and Maggie seven years ago when we buried Dad. And I saw Maggie again yesterday when we buried Mam. The sight at Mam's graveside chilled me to the core.

Maggie was standing there, wearing Gran's forget-me-not ring. And, although there was nothing strange in that, as I beheld her appearance, a shiver ran the length of my body: I was ten years old again.

Maggie's wispy streaked hair was swept across her scalp, clamped with a clip. I looked into her face and she held my gaze. It was not the expression of a young woman I saw before me, but the glacial stare of an 86-year-old pair of eyes.

Acknowledgements

On behalf of Word Machine Press, a tremendous thank you goes out to the following. Without your generosity, this book would not have been possible:

Shari Altman, Colin Anderson, Helen Anderson, Iain Anderson, Tricia Anderson, Alison Ashlin, Lulu Badger, Gill Bannerman, Annie Batchelor, Judith Batey, Amanda Benson, Igor Bosisio, Casey Bottono, Mark Bould, Colin Bradbury, Stephen Branfield, Helen Bridgewater, Suzanne Louise Brooks, Shari Brown, Bonnie Charles, Danielle Charles, Ryan Charles, Emma Chilcott, Charles Colchester, Christine Collar, Clare Mary Corcoran, Charlotte Crofts, Barbara Crosby, Katie Crosby, Catherine Crossland, Eleanor Crossland, Liz Crossland, Michael Davies, Robbie Dixon, Kervin Martínez Dockendorf, Jill Doctor, Paul Dodgson, Marina Dunford, Caroline Eyles, Victoria Field, Alison Fixsen, Rebecca Fox, Lucy Frears, Miranda Freeborn-Swan, Patrick Gale, James Gioia, Ingrid Grylls, Judith Gutmanis, Lynn Hill, Andrew Houston, Louisa Hughes, Linda Kelso, Wade L. Kelso, Kris Kenway, Peter Kimball-Evans, Jenny Knight, Daniel Kubinski, John Lake, Rebecca M. LaTocha, J. Levang, Stein Roald Levang, Tim Levang, Graham Lewis, Corrina Lowry, Christopher James Lyall, David McCormick, Patrick McEvoy, Susan McGowan, Andrea McNamara, Liz Meierr, Pam Meiklejohn, Dawn Mellor, Meish Melnyczuk, Mike Melnyczuk, Val Melnyczuk, Euan Monaghan, Simo Muinonen,

Paul Mulraney, Donna Painter, Jennifer Parker, Catherine Pettitt, Julie Podesky, Dominic Power, Richard Rapley, Libby Reed, Jennifer Roberts, Jeannie Robinson, Jonathan Robinson, Jesse Rowe, Kenneth Salmon, Karyn Schwartz, Tom Scott, Janet Shaw, Alma Shearer, Andrew Shearer, Colin Shearer, Joanne Shearer, Kenn Shearer, Pauline Shearer, Stephen Shearer, Anton Shepelev, Helen Shipman, John Simmons, Lis Sinclair, Abigail Sitch, Trystan Spalding-Jenkin, Zack Spencer, Nicky Stephenson, Tania, Helen Thomas, Michael James, Peter Thonger, Roger Thorp, Jessica Tompkins, Downward Viral, Jason Vowles, Tina Walker, Lucinda Warner, Gregory Wellington, Katie Weselby, Andreas Harald Wild, Simon Woodhall.

Illustrators

Fiona Rose Batey
Cover, *The Inheritance* and *The Bypass*

Bethan Ford
Vivienne, Bladderwrack and *Forget-Me-Not*

Jenny Levang
Lost Soul, Shadow Play and *The Ghosts of Havisham Manor*

Debbie Phillips
Word Machine Press logo design

All illustrations copyright 2013